THE DEPTHS OF LOVE

AN SFWG ANTHOLOGY

Published by:
Cloaked Press, LLC
PO Box 341
Suring, WI 54174
http://www.cloakedpress.com

Cover Design by:
Fantasy & Coffee Design
https://fantasyandcoffee.com/SPDesign/

ISBN: 978-1-952796-01-2

THE SCI-FI & FANTASY WRITERS' GUILD PRESENTS:

M.A. ROBERTS

R.Q. WOODWARD

LOWRY POLETTI

N.R. WILLIAMS

MARK J. SCHULTIS

BETHANY A. PERRY

R.A. MEENAN

BRANDON FIFE

M.D. WEATHER

IGNACIO R. LIMÓN

SUSAN ESCHBACH

CLEMENTINE FRASER

ANDREW M. FERRELL

CONTENTS

FOREWORD

It has been my biggest project for the last five years to run the Sci-Fi & Fantasy Writers' Guild with the help of so many wonderful admins and moderators. We set out to make a community of writers, dedicated toward unity, respect, and growth, and we found that, together.

I look forward to more great anthologies, and great years together. To those reading, enjoy! Come find hope, love, and humanity in the least expected of places.

-Mato J. Steger

FOUNDER OF SFWG
www.sfwritersguild.com

CHILDREN OF THE SEA

M.A. ROBERTS

Never trust a fairy godmother. The other mer warned her that all humans were like the fishermen, deceitful and cruel, but this old woman smelled of coral and kelp, trustworthy things. And she looked so lost, hunched beneath a parasol in her sad little boat while the sharp morning sun baked her brown, leathery skin. The mermaid took pity on her, but nothing, especially the help of a mer, came for free. So they struck a bargain, a favor for a favor. She swam alongside the boat, leading it back to shore. The trip was easy for her, but the woman grumbled as she rowed and demanded to be towed by a rope. A rope in the sea...the thought made the mer shudder, but towing was not a part of their bargain. It took all morning and much of the afternoon, but she led the woman to shore as she promised. In exchange for her help, the fairy godmother gave her legs for the rest of the day and a beautiful, seafoam dress that shimmered like the waves.

They parted ways at the beach and never once did the mermaid question why the woman stayed in the boat and rowed back out to sea. She tottered away on wobbly legs, growing queasy when the too silky skin of her thighs brushed together. At first, she struggled to keep her balance, but soon she was marching along the shoreline, sand crunching under her feet, the loose grains scratching between her toes.

Confident she wouldn't fall on her face, the mermaid set off to discover how humans lived. There had to be more to them than their sharp hooks and strong nets. Oh she knew the myths. The mer told tales of a human world full of delights, exotic foods, warm fires, dancers and musicians and acrobats and storytellers. All wonderful things, and all of them lies designed to draw you in like the lures the fishermen used to catch and kill. But she had seen other people out on their boats, laughing, having fun with their families. Yes, fishermen were evil, but surely not all humans were. She wanted to see the truth of them for herself.

The tide was high, barely past its peak as she found the road and began the short walk into town. She had hours left before the new day, but halfway there, the magic ran out. Her legs clamped together. The mermaid toppled, her shoulder crashing against the hard-packed earth. The skin stretched and fused as it grew sharp, iridescent scales. Her feet elongated, morphing into fins, and her lovely dress dissolved, leaving nothing but shells and seaweed to cover herself with. She thrashed and clawed her way off the road. Her lips thinned and turned back to blue as she cursed the fairy godmother for her trickery, but most of all, she cursed herself for being a fool for even she knew humans judge the day by the sun and not the tides.

She stared back at the water. So close. Less than a league but she struggled even to crawl off the road. The water might as well be a thousand leagues away.

"Help!"

She cried out, over and over, but no one listened. No

one stopped. No one cared. As the dusk faded into night, dozens of people passed her, their boots kicking up dust, leaving her parched and coughing, but only one or two ever glanced her way. Each time she met their eyes, hope stirred. Surely, someone would take pity on her, but while some gawked and sniggered, none of them uttered a word to her or listened to her pleas. It seemed their hearts were as cold and hard as the metal hooks they plunged into the sea.

After a time, she quit begging. She curled her body around her tail and cried, hot saltwater tears rolling down her cheeks.

An hour passed. The sun kissed the horizon, and the sky bled, yellow and pink spilling between the clouds.

A sailor, far from home and the woman he loved, wandered toward the town from the shore. He hoped to find strong drinks and reasonably priced affection, but when he spotted the mermaid, he stopped to stare. The moonlight shimmered on silver scales and cast an orange hue over smooth pale flesh. Hearing him, she stirred, sitting up and tucking her tail beneath her.

"Please," she implored, "carry me back to the sea. I'll catch fish for you. I'll swim alongside your ship and warn you of dangers."

He scoffed. "Would you return me to land if you found me in the water? No, you would drown me, so I'll not help you."

The sailor stepped back, but he didn't leave. His eyes drifted down, admiring her shells. But she was a beast, not a person. Later, on particularly lonely nights, he would touch himself and think of her, but he would never stoop so low as to touch a monster. The mermaid flopped onto her belly and buried her face in her arms. The sailor lingered until he had his fill of pale skin and soft curves.

Much later, as the moon reached its zenith and her fluttering gills dried and cracked, a young witch in a brand-new pointy hat strode down the road. The woman bounced and bubbled, a broad smile on her face and a skip in her step. The mermaid rolled to her back and propped herself up on trembling arms. Perhaps a happy person would return her to the sea.

"Help me, please." Her tail twitched, and she slapped it against the ground to stop herself from fidgeting. "I'll teach you to breathe underwater, and I'll bring you treasures from the ocean floor."

The witch already had her hat, her magic, and a talking frog. She wanted nothing from the sea and trusted nothing this sea creature said. Chin held high, she stared down her crooked nose at the fish who thought she was a woman and sniffed. But as she turned to leave, the mermaid whimpered. Her weary head dipped, and moonlight swam through her hair, highlighting a hundred swirling shades of blue and green. The young witch drew her knife and rushed forward. She grabbed a fist full of teal hair and jerked the mermaid's head to one side. The blade hacked through cobalt, azure, and sapphire, leaving a jagged patchwork of uneven tufts and a thin trickle of blood running down the creature's forehead.

A sliver of unicorn horn and a single strand of turquoise hair stolen from a mermaid in distress, made the best wands in the world. With the right spell, the extra hair would make beautiful bristles for a broom. Now, the witch really did own everything she needed. A hat, a wand, a broom, and a talking frog, what more could she want? She skipped away, never seeing the mermaid's tears or giving the poor creature a second thought.

A cool breeze blew in from the sea, flowing over her scales and fins, but it brought no relief. And as the night stretched, the number of townspeople passing dwindled to almost nothing, but the chef worked late every night and was always the last one out on the streets. He loved his job. Lately though, he grew tired of the local mongers hawking nothing but salmon, cod, and muscles. He wanted to cook a swordfish, a shark, or a whale. Something new, something exciting, so when he spotted the mermaid, face pressed to the dirt on the side of the road, his mouth watered. He wondered what sauce went best with mermaid. Perhaps something creamy with a hint of lemon, or, if she were still fresh, he would serve her raw, sliced thin and drizzled with ginger and lime.

He hurried across the road and nudged her side with the toe of his boot, intending to roll her over, but she groaned. Heart leaping into his throat, he stumbled back as her head lifted. Desperate eyes found his.

"Help," she whispered, soft and raspy.

"You're alive!"

She reached for him, and he jumped back. Salmon. He quite liked salmon wrapped in paper and baked with lemons and herbs. Best of all, salmon never talked to him. She sniffled as he scurried off, his head filling with dreams of orca steaks and narwhal pies.

The mermaid closed her eyes, too exhausted to call out after him.

The fog rolled in, moist and soothing, and rain fell, washing away the dust. She relaxed beneath the gentle patter, expecting a moment of relief, but the freshwater stole her salt and burned her scales. Dark clouds gathered overhead, and fat drops, hard as hail, pelted her back and head. She braced against the bitter sting and crawled toward the only shelter in sight, a stout wooden cart on the other side of the road. Her elbows dug into the earth, churning dirt into mud, and the whole mess clung to her, weighing her down and searing her flesh. She flopped and wiggled until the rain swept under the cart and carried it away. With no other options left, she lay back in the muck, endured the pain, and waited for whatever came next.

She woke before the sun, brought to by the butt of a fishing rod prodding her stomach. A night full of cold and storms left her shivering and bruised, and the new day promised nothing but pain and humiliation. She squeezed her eyes tight and waited for the human to laugh or torment her. She didn't care, so long as it left her alone to die in

5

peace.

"A mermaid stuck on land?" A man's bare foot tapped against her fins. "You must have a quite interesting tale."

"I..." She rolled to her back and blinked up at him. "Was that meant to be funny?"

A laugh rumbled through his chest and out his nose. He didn't joke often, but right now, strong coffee and seven rashers of bacon warmed his stomach. It would be hours yet before he turned into the grouchy old man of the sea.

She huffed and wiped the sleep from her eyes. Only then did she recognize the rod and reel. Her exhaustion evaporated, and she flailed, trying to crawl away. The man's smile sagged at the corners as a full rasher's worth of happiness disappeared.

"Am I that ugly?" he asked.

"You're a fisherman!"

"And you're an evil sea demon, or so people say."

"At least I don't snare innocent mer in traps. How would you like it if I hung hooks in your home and tore your flesh?" She held up an arm, showing him the crooked scar running from her elbow to her wrist.

"And I don't drown people for doing an honest day's work."

Her gills flared. "I would never —"

"Do you want my help or not?" he asked.

The mermaid stilled, waiting to hear the catch or the rest of the cruel joke. She knew little of humans but knew fishermen were the cruelest of them all.

"Come on," he said. "Let's get you back to the ocean."

"Why would you help me?"

"That's never been my home." He gestured toward the town then out to the ocean. "The sea is my mother as surely as she is yours, and she loves you. Helping you is what she'd want."

She almost laughed. The fishermen waged war against those in the water and he thought of himself as a son of the sea.

"We are not family. I cut your nets and sink your boats."

"And I hang hooks in your home." He shrugged. "Family ain't always nice. Da's brother once sank my boat too. Too much drink and too little sense, and some old anger about the time I burned down his outhouse. Still, he's family, and I wouldn't leave him to die in the mud either. Though, I might let him squirm a bit first."

He laughed and jogged off to fetch the cart. His knees creaked and groaned as he loaded her into the back, more carefully than she expected. She bit her tongue and resisted the urge to fight. Right now, she must take any chance of help no matter who offered it. A quarter of an hour later, the wheels sank into sand and stuck. He grunted, pushing to no avail, but she didn't notice. The roar and smack of waves lapping against the shore demanded her attention. Home, and just a few hundred yards away. She squeaked when he lifted her from the cart, but he was gentle as he trudged across the beach and laid her in his boat. Despite her weakness and the strong tide rolling in, she longed to leap from his arms and swim away. Instead, she waited, tail twitching. Every mermaid knew better than to fight the ocean.

The old man muttered about his age as he worked the oars, but they dipped and swept with a practiced grace. She cupped her hands in the sea and splashed salty water over her face and gills. Soon, they crested the last of the waves and floated on a smooth, calm ocean. She turned to thank him, but something slammed into the underside of the boat, tossing her overboard.

Relief washed over her as she sank beneath the surface. The ocean welcomed her, soothing her dry scales, but someone grabbed her and yanked her away as the fisherman splashed into the water. Long, slender fingers brushed through her short, ragged hair, and her sister's voice whispered in her mind.

"*What did he do to you?*"

"*Nothing.*" She tried to pull away, but she was still so

weak. Strong arms held her in a tight embrace while a dozen mer circled their target.

"*The fishermen have gone too far this time.*"

The mer shot through the water, closing the distance. The man kicked and clawed, struggling to reach the surface, but they grabbed him and held him tight.

They hadn't seen the fairy godmother or her trickery. She went missing and they found her battered and bruised, her hair hacked off and her scales flaking. And they found her with a fisherman. Of course they assumed he did it. He was the enemy, the worst of all humans.

He looked to her, eyes wide as he gagged, sucking water instead of air.

The worst of all humans but he listened. He cared. None of the others had. They were as hard as the stone they built their homes from, but he said those weren't his home.

"*No! It wasn't him!*" She squirmed, trying to reach the others but her sister held her back.

She cried out, over and over, but no one listened. No one stopped. No one cared. They dragged him deeper into the dark water until he disappeared and the tiny bubbles of breath burbling up to the surface died. Her sister tried to hug her, but the mermaid pushed away, curling her body around her tail and crying, hot saltwater tears for a son of the sea.

WOODBINE

R.Q. WOODWARD

Some say I bring fortune, good will or riches untold. Others claim I act as a ward, cleansing toxic air or preventing malevolence from coming near. Boon or remedy, I know not.

All I know is that I was a gift.

A gift to a small, sweet thing with delicate hands and a gentle voice. Her bare feet race across the grass, while I stay rooted. The little girl dances and plays in her homespun clothes. I stretch my limbs toward the sky.

We grow together.

In the summer, trumpet-like white and yellow flowers bloom from my vines, and my darling girl coos with delight. She adores me. Bees admire me too. They drift near my darling, but I shoo them away, never letting a single sting harm her.

I am safety.

I am luck.

The sun burns bright, shriveling the once green grass. My darling is ever attentive, inspecting my branches and watering my roots. Another voice, wizened with age, instructs her on how best to do so. My florescence fades.

When the weather turns and trees shed their leaves, I remain steady. I bear it all: the wind, driving rain, and sleet. My nectar filled flowers may be gone, but my leaves, my vines, my roots endure.

Snow catches on my limbs. It clings to me and blankets the ground. For the first time, I understand fear.

For I am young.

The cherub child tends to me. She replaces my white shroud with cozy wood chips and clears ice from my vines. The older voice, female, educates on this topic too.

The child—no, *my* child—protects me through winter. She is vigilant, my fiercest champion, and I vow to be hers.

When the ground thaws, new buds dazzle my branches. My child too has changed. She is taller, smarter, stronger than when we first were given to each other. The days turn warm, and we grow in chorus once more.

And so it continues year by year. The seasons change. We change, each sprouting in our own distinct and beautiful ways.

Until a carriage arrives to take my child away. She is as tall as her mother now, with knobby ankles and wrists peeking from the edges of her threadbare dress. A maid's cap rests on her head like a crown. In her eyes, excitement and fear mingle with unshed tears. She caresses my leaves in parting. I wish she would take me with her, pluck a single flower to carry on her bosom. But she does not. My child, my lovely daughter, leaves me.

I know not where she goes. Only that she is gone.

Seasons pass.

I bloom every spring, but my daughter does not return to pluck my blossoms or taste the sweet honey inside.

My shoots are longer now. The woman who remains in

10

the house clips them and twines them together to make rope. With her delicate touch, the sting is minimal. I am glad to be of use. She gleans my blooms and slips them beneath her pillow to ensure pleasant dreams. I gift her with whimsical fantasies of my daughter.

Her daughter, I suppose.

Our daughter.

The two of us fall into a new rhythm. I guard the front wall of her home—keeping evil spirits away while I nurture her garden—and she tends to me, as attentive as our daughter would be.

I am safety.

I *am* luck.

In late winter, when my vines are just beginning to wake, my child returns. She is no longer a child though. She is a woman with a swaddled babe in her arms and a horrifying story on her lips. A brutal story. One of cruelty and pain. One of tragedy and injustice.

My vines twist and quake with anger for my precious child. For her precious child. Three in all now.

I have three daughters.

One very young. One somewhat old. All three are mine. And I will protect them with life and limb.

My daughters weep together. They pack bundles and soothe the babe to keep her quiet. They will flee. My hopes and well wishes will be with them always, but I fear that is not enough.

As my oldest daughter steps from her lifelong home, I snag on her skirts. She comes to me.

With a practiced hand, she takes a clipping. I am severed, broken in two. But I will be strong, just as my first daughter, the young mother, was. I will survive, same as all three of my dear ones.

I will protect them.

Days pass. I rest alone in the darkness. Frantic whispers and anxious fretting over the babe both concern and relieve me. They are safe, for now.

In the dead of night, silent and still but for a lonely owl hooting in the distance, my roots meet new soil. I awaken with the dawn. My roots nestle the earth beside the doorway of a new house. A cottage with tightly closed shutters. We are far away from our old home.

Still, the women are wary. One daughter wants to keep apart from our new neighbors, while the other believes allies can be made among them. I will safeguard my cherished ones no matter what they decide.

The months turn hot, but I am too young to flower. Each vine I sprout, my daughters prune and plant. With their help, I line the entire front side of the cottage, meager shoots barely tall enough to greet the sun.

They will nurture me, and I will thrive. I will shelter my daughters and bring all three luck and wealth as the years pass.

Fate willing.

News arrives of a group of foreigners searching for a missing babe.

"They say she is a princess," a neighbor whispers.

"I recall no royal announcement," my eldest daughter says.

"The Queen did not share...in the making, it is said."

My oldest daughter sends the neighbor away, expression bleak. Next, my daughters gather their possessions, topple the lone chair they have acquired, throw dirt and ashes over every surface. They flee. My heart goes with them, but my diminutive vines and roots cannot. I remain firmly embedded in the soil.

The men arrive. They stomp, and they swear. They search the chimney and rip apart the mattress. They smash the chair and dislodge shutters from the windows.

When the foreigners depart, clumsy feet crush several of my newly planted vines.

I will die here, untended. I am not like my cousins, the wild woodbine, able to twist and tangle hairy branches through any obstruction. That variety of honeysuckle brings ill luck when carried inside homes.

Not I.

I am luck.

I am sanctuary.

I am security.

But I must be wanted.

The sun greets me thrice, and I wither beneath its rays. The ground is dry. My short roots ache and shrivel. The part of me that was trampled lies flat on the ground, dying.

In the middle of the night, a gentle hand brushes my leaves. Water soaks into the quenched parts of me. My daughters have returned.

My spirit rises high, high, high. I stretch my limbs to match it.

As the women set their house in order, clearing what was ruined and repairing what was not, I grow and thrive. My daughters bend my vines to the side and replant them each day, twice a day, until I am wrapped thrice around the cottage, ample and waist high. My limbs crisscross and knit.

More than vine, I am bramble.

I am brush. A bulwark for their new home.

The weather turns cool, and I flower. The young mother smiles and sips of my honey as she did when she was a child. Bees lavish me with kisses. A pair of birds build a nest in my shrubbery. I will guard them all.

Brown and orange leaves litter the barren ground, and over them come the crunch, crunch, crunch of new feet. The men are back. They pound on the door while my daughter and her babe steal through a back window, dropping noiselessly into my arms. A flower slides over the young mother's forehead. She breathes in its scent and goes still, so very still.

Inside, the men shout. They ask harsh questions, and my eldest daughter weaves a cunning tale, soothing the ruffians with honeyed words.

Within my arms, the babe stirs but does not cry out. I

press a kiss to her brow as I did to her mother.

They are safe here.

Well into the night, after the men are gone, my daughters remain in my embrace. I shield them from the cold, night air and cushion their exhausted bodies. When the old woman seeks them, I lift the pair from my arms and place them in hers. They retreat indoors with muffled sobs. My desire to shelter them stretches my arms higher.

As the first snows blanket the earth, I climb to the eaves of the cottage, and extend my fingers. I push through powder and ice, shivering as my blossoms fall, invisible, onto a white, crystalline bed. I grow, and grow, and grow, until the entire cottage is encased in my shrubbery. I stretch and bend to cover the door and windows. My daughters may pass through unhindered, but none other shall.

I am protection.

I am refuge.

When the men return a third time, I am ready. Instead of a cottage, they find a snow-covered hill. They spin and scratch their heads, looking for what stands right before them. Snowflakes whirl in the sky. The fading light sends them onward. From my perch high upon the roof, I can see where they build their camp. A fire burns all night despite the wind licking its flames.

In the morn, the men renew their search. A few heads turn in my direction before looking away to continue the hunt. They tromp through knee-high snow as fresh flakes litter their shoulders. Winter wind howls and rips at my vines, but I hold firm.

The storm eases. Their campfire is sizable and brighter in the gloomy darkness of night. Frigid air seeps between my vines, chilling me to the core and wilting my leaves. A thin tendril of smoke curls up from the cottage chimney. I can keep my daughters hidden, but I cannot keep them warm.

Golden rays light the sky as the last of the chimney smoke scatters in the wind. Its fragrance lingers, and even my blossoms cannot conceal the scent.

A shout rings out. Then another.

Men encircle the house. One attempts to climb. Another tugs at my frozen limbs. Inside, the babe begins to cry.

Wide eyes turn to one another, and it begins.

Axes chop and hack at my vines. Fingers mangle and pull. Aching, throbbing, hurting, I am torn apart bit by bit.

I recall the story my daughter told, of ravishing. Of violating. Of bruising and suffering, desecrated by the merciless hands of another.

The assault comes from every direction. Branches rip. Leaves scatter. Moisture bleeds from every part of me they touch. They do not temper their torture. They are relentless. My agony persists as they force my roots from the ground. They destroy me, utterly and completely.

My petals weep.

I am undone.

The cottage is exposed, its front door revealed. The roots of my original vines are beaten and trampled as the men assail the entryway. Like me, the door is torn apart.

Screams and wails rend the bleeding sky, and my ravaged body is left scattered in the snow.

I am devastated.

I am razed.

The men leave with victory on their tongues, singing songs of their recovered princess. My princess. They have taken her. My precious daughter, no more than a babe.

Fury twists my broken vines. Splintered edges harden into thorns. They shall not have her.

A winter gale lifts snow and more from the ground. My fractured pieces fly through the sky, spiraling and swooping as they follow the men. The group pauses in the center of the village to announce their triumph. My wailing daughter is lifted into the freezing air, and they cheer.

I am fury.

I am wrath.

The gale reaches the party, lifting hats from heads and

bending backs. My branches mask their eyes. Vines snake around throats and squeeze. I bind hands and feet, press thorns deep into chests. Flowers cascade from the sky like giant snowflakes, surrounding the hoard with an intoxicating fragrance. Mine will be the last scent they breathe.

My daughter falls, but I catch her, soft pieces of me weaving together so fast they may as well have never been broken. I am a basket, a blanket, a pillow to brace her fall.

I am all of these things and none of them at once. For I was severed from my roots, and I am dying. My daughter coos as I kiss her forehead with a blossom for the final time.

I am comfort.

I am calm.

Townsfolk crowd around to see the havoc I have wreaked, friendly faces among them. My leaves crunch underfoot, and brittle branches snap. I will die here, a ruined wreck of what I once was, but I am fulfilled. My daughter is secure in my arms, and none shall harm her. I will hold her and imbue her with my blessing.

For I am woodbine.

I am safety.

I am luck.

I RETURNED IN
THE NIGHT

LOWRY POLETTI

The dragon's unblinking eyes stare toward the sky. My skin burns where he touched me, where his claws held me in the wet embrace of the marsh. I let the point of my sword fall to my feet.

It is Diarseig who you will kill, the priest said to me weeks ago. *The immortal dragon that haunts the forest.*

A hand falls on my shoulder. I tear myself away, grip tightening around my sword, but only one of the town's farmers stands before me. He drops his knife when he sees my face. When he and his lot led me to the wood, had he expected Diarseig to come two inches from snapping my neck or for his teeth to scratch a bloody line down the side of my face? The knights in their folktales always slayed the beast untouched.

I had been sent because the dragon intruded on their

lands and left the bones of their cattle at the threshold of the woods—surely, they reasoned, a man would be next, trapped in the cage of Diarseig's throat.

"Sir knight?" the farmer asks. The others stay behind him, scraped up but otherwise unharmed. The dragon focused his attentions on me, and I have the dents in my armor to prove it. I hazard a glance to the side where the dagger stuck in Diarsieg's eye catches the setting sunlight.

When he held me down, his eyes shone like citrines, and he looked at me as if he recognized my face. The taste of his blood, like tree sap, now sits in my mouth.

I turn to the rest of the men.

"Go back to your homes," I say, loud enough to scare away a flock of birds. "Diarseig is slain."

They hesitate. One points to the corpse, and several whisper frantically.

I follow their eyes. The dragon's belly churns as if his flesh is boiling beneath the skin. His black scales have an oily sheen which slipped into the shadows like an otter might slip into the surface of a lake. I put a hand on the leathery skin, and I'm struck with the desire for him to live, still, and for his eyes to meet mine once more.

I shove my sword into his belly. His yellow blood pools around the blade with the translucent viscosity of syrup. Another tear, and his guts spill around my feet.

The few men behind me recoil. Upon a nest of intestines sits a mesentery pouch of gelatinous orbs. I lower myself until I am level with one of the embryos within: a fetal serpent, as long as a finger, curled around a mass of veins and still.

Nearly half a year ago, I sit in the dusty shadows of my home, the monastery. Sour sweat and sand coat my tongue.

Sir Vivian Alba sits across from me, his hand palm-up

within mine. A gash runs across his skin, nearly black from the grit. He stumbled over his own feet when I advanced on him and tried to catch himself on an ill-repaired wall. Blood rarely graces the ground of this courtyard, but now it dots it like jewels. Our abandoned staves lie there.

I dab at his hand with a rag wet with liquor. I already fumbled my way through apologies, recited lines of repentance in my head—while he cursed and then laughed at my embarrassment, bloodied hand displayed beside his face. Now we hold ourselves in a simple silence, and I can enjoy the satisfying ache that drags at my muscles as if to pull me into the earth. Such are the fruits of sparring with a man of equal mettle; this, and the music of his panting and the sweat that drips down his brow.

Alcohol seeps into the wound. His lips curl upward when he hissed, catching at the scar on his cheek.

"Sir Alba?"

"How many times have I told you?" he says. His eyes, so hazel that they are nearly yellow, are level with mine.

I stumble over my words. "It is a habit—"

"How many times?" Then he says his name slowly, so I can watch his tongue click against his upper teeth.

"Vivian," I repeat. "You'll need to keep this clean."

The hem of his trousers brushes against my ankle as he shifts closer. We wear nearly identical clothing—the same undyed muslin, bound at the waist, and quilted cotton fastened at each shoulder—distinguishable only by the hastily mended tears that mar Vivian's tunic. I have known him for so long that we could have the same skin, too, issued by the King and branded with the white bird of God.

I press too close to the wound. At the touch, his skin gapes apart and a new trickle of translucent liquid rises to the surface. Vivian flinches away, a low noise in the back of his throat.

An apology rises to my mouth, but he looks me straight in the eye. He's laughing again, and this laugh ends in a hoarse cough, smothered against the back of his good hand.

He clears his throat instead. The wind slicks back his hair, oil-slick black.

"I've been hurt worse, you know," he says, half a smile on his lips. He leans closer. His hand is scaled with callouses and familiar to me. I trace the lines of his palm from memory.

"You can have Maria help you with the dressing." I know his wife, and she will worry. She has experience nursing after her sister, also, who succumbed to blackburn fever some years prior.

He grins, full of teeth. "Maria? No, I think I am going to stay the night. Look."

His eyes roll upward; so do mine. Storm clouds drift over a graying sky, visible through the courtyard's open roof. I imagine him wet with rainwater, mouth full of water and skin slick.

"It'll be dark soon," he says. "And I'd hate to walk so far in the rain."

I return in the night to that place. My torch throws orange light across the darkened marsh trees.

The smell of the dragon's body hangs in the air. Even if I didn't remember the way, I would still be able to find him.

As I approach, the ground squelches underfoot and the air trickles down my throat. I hesitate at the sight of the corpse in the distance, broken by peeling birches. My bruises ache with a new ferocity, and the scratches along my cheek burn. I continue until I stand before him.

Diarseig's body had collapsed into the earth, and seeing his face, I remind myself that he is dead. His cavernous bones jut from the ground like the shards of a rotting tree trunk. In fish-like layers, his muscles peel away. The air about him is too warm, too full of water; yet his mouth lies open to grin at me and his single eye reflects the shadows of the leafy canopy. When I see this mouth, I think of Vivian's voice cradling my name.

I don't hold his gaze. Instead, I inspect the eggs.

Many of them have already disintegrated, eaten in part by worms. At my approach, a wild dog looks up with flashing eyes. The limp body of a serpent dangles from its jaws. Its nostrils flare before it flees.

Pressing the end of my torch into the dirt, I go to one knee. One of the eggs remains whole. It wobbles as I cup it between two hands. Blue veins connect the fetus to its yolk. Even suspended in jelly, the creature squirms away from my light.

I slide the egg into the cotton sack on my waist and turn back to the house.

"Sir?"

I hesitate in the hall. The smell of rosemary and cloves is so thick that it makes my eyes water. I have the monastery memorized, each altar and each intersecting hall, but this is new to me. The air sits as thick as after-rain fog, and the sound of coughing echoes out from a single open door.

"He's been asking after you, sir."

This acolyte that stands before me—he's tall and as spindly as a bundle of twigs. He holds his arms in front of himself and fixes me with a blue-tinged gaze. Both his mouth and nose are covered in a soaked cloth, warding away the miasma.

"I'm sorry?" I say. Absently, he hands me a similar rag, which sits dead in my palm. His young face is so serious that he appears older and grayed.

"Sir, he won't—"

The coughing rises higher as if Vivian's lungs are bellows, his ribcage the expansive arch of a hearth. I turn away. My hands dig at my collarbone, struggling to find purchase against the satin. I imagine his deathbed, cloaked in incense and stained yellow with phlegm. Does the doctor's hand sit on his bare back, along the ladder of his emaciated spine? Are his arms dotted with leeches? I watched him, in just a matter of weeks, fade away to bones and skin.

"Where is his wife?" I ask.

"He turned her away. He said—"

"*Where is Maria?*"

When have I ever spoken so loudly? The sound of my own voice makes my ears ache.

"He asked for you." The acolyte presses his lips tight, but his eyes are still a hairsbreadth too wide. "Sir—"

My name rings out, then, in a voice so ragged that it crawls along the floor. A shudder runs through my body and for a moment, I can't breathe.

"Please." It's the same voice, interrupted by another wet hack. He's drowning from the inside out. "Please, find him."

Like this, I am summoned. Rag pressed to my nose, I bring myself beside his door, where the shadow of the doctor stretches across the threshold. I stop there. I can't see him.

I put my ear to the wall as if his unmarred voice might meet me, should I listen carefully enough.

I can't bring myself to take another step or to breathe that fouled air. The man inside is hardly a man and thinking of his gray skin stretched across the hollow of his cheeks makes pain spread across my chest.

He says my name again, softly in his wheezing exhale. My blood runs cold at the realization that he has heard me or that he has noticed my shadow at the foot of his door.

I tear myself away.

"Wait!" High-pitched air whistles above his cries. "I know you're there!"

I gesture the acolyte over. "Have his wife summoned again, and Father Michael. Place his sword at his side for his final rites. He will have it no other way."

"*Please!*" Vivian says, and my name, again, claws at the ceiling in a scream. The acolyte grimaces.

"Sir, shouldn't you...?"

"Are you listening to me?" My voice is a hiss, my face lowered to the acolyte's. Excuses, lies fill my mouth—anything to explain away my own cowardice. "He is not in his right mind. You know this."

"You can't leave," Vivian cries.

The acolyte nods. "Of course, sir."

"Should I die alone?" he says to me. "Because of you?"

I look at the light streaming out from his room a single time before I turn back down the hall. Between his words, he gasps so violently for air that I can hear this, also. The sound makes me want to tear the skin from my hands.

"*You coward!*"

I reach the end of the hall, where I lean against the corner and dig furrows in the grout.

"If you leave—" He dogs me. "—I'll hate you with every breath until I die, and after, too. I swear it. I'll dig myself out of my grave and back to you. I'll haunt you until there is nothing left at all."

In the days after his death, Diarseig fills my dreams. I stand in the forest and the bitter cold makes my skin feverish.

The dragon finds me, and I stumble away. I think that he is here to kill me. Roots press against my heels as if to grab me. I smell oak sap so clearly that I wonder if I'm awake.

I say, "You're dead."

His head tilts to the side. He holds his body low to the ground. Beneath his stomach sits a mound of eggs, untouched. These are guarded by a white serpent—I saw the same serpent drawn in the texts that foretold Diarseig's arrival.

"You, out of anyone," he says, "should know that the dead can speak."

I shake my head. If Diarseig is here, then I have failed. If a dead beast is here, then another ghost may still lurk here.

He stretches closer to me. His heated breath blusters against my chest. His mouth falls open just an inch so I can see the glowing red between his teeth.

"What do you think he would do to you?" Diarseig asks. "If he were here?"

"He would kill me."

Diarseig hums low in his throat.

"He *will* kill me," I say again.

But the dragon is already gone. When I wake, I smell tree sap, sand and sweat. I check my hands for blood, but they are clean. The room spins around me when I stand. I plunge my hands into a basin of water at my bedside. They are still clean. I look up and the eyes in the wooden boards stare back at me. I dig at the skin beneath my nails, but this too is clean. The chill of the water has worked its way up my arm with needle-pricks of numbness. I imagine myself without hands at all, chapped skin pale with scars, so I don't imagine a warrior's palm torn and bleeding.

To think that I have not escaped this fear, even after Diarseig's death, fills me with a silent resignation.

With an intake of breath, I press my hands beneath my shirt until the cloth soaks up the water, and I sink against the wall. There, I watch the door to my cabin until morning.

I keep Diarseig's egg in a bowl of stream water. In the stillness of the glass, I see my own reflection: my elfin face hardened and scarred, my long hair coated in grime, my eyes oil-paint dark.

Over the week, the fetus tripled in size, its budding limbs folded neatly against its body. Now only a thin layer of jelly separates it from the outside world.

I sit beside its small table. While I am stationed here, the townspeople have sequestered me in an abandoned house on the outskirts of town. It is so similar to my cell in the monastery that the sight of the darkening walls turns my stomach.

I have just a few more days out here, in the untouched forests. Just a few days with this new discovery.

Movement catches my eye. I run a nail down the glass bowl. The fetus within stirs. It arches its back, like a kitten stretching, and the membrane splits apart. One stray claw lands on the edge of the bowl, and with monumental effort, it pulls its uncoordinated body halfway out of the water. Its eyes widen at the sight of me, and me at it. Its sideways eyelids blink once, twice, then three times.

I hold out my hand. It wiggles its way onto my palm and wraps its tail around my forearm. It has black scales like its father, and these glitter faintly. I did not expect it to be so lovely—but I did not expect Diarseig to be so lovely, either. A warmth spreads through my chest.

I lower it back to its bowl, where it dips into the water with a fluttering splash.

In the first five days after the death of Sir Vivian Alba, I do not eat. I tear the hair from my head and offer it to God's doves. I spend my nights awake, sure that I'll see his hand slide beneath my door in the moonlight, sure that he will invade my dreams. In the delirium of hunger and fatigue, I wish that he would.

A gray haze falls across the monastery in this time. I drag myself to the altar at the request of my betters, but I see his face in the shadows of the pews, in the flickering of the candles lined across the stone tables.

"You've been summoned," the priest says, a book clutched between his gloved hands, "to slay a dragon."

"I'm sorry, Father, but I—"

"Worry not. You will have ample time to build your strength once more. After all, you are quite the accomplished hunter."

I know he is thinking of my last quest, at Vivian's side, where we tracked a great wolf to its lair and cut from its belly the head of a young girl. My stomach turns.

He gestures forward with a wave of his elaborate sleeve, candlelight playing at the gray of his hair. With a whispered prayer, he places the book on the altar. "Here, look."

I do, and I listen as his finger draws across the page.

"They say that he hatches from the earth, a serpent, and drinks the blood of the innocent until he is bloated and fully formed. In fact, they contacted us a few months ago with the same rumor—that a local girl had seen a black serpent in the grass, six feet long and round with a deer in its belly. Of course, we dismissed this as a—" The priest pauses. "— a stroke of fancy. But the dragon they describe now is strikingly similar to our records."

He shows me a page in a book where a black salamander coils among wild grass, split in twain by a fanciful sword. He turns the page. The beast's claws sprawl across the page, and a white serpent coils between its feet.

"He is Diarseig," he says to me. "The demon that haunts the forest, and he is reborn."

I think: *This is it. This is he, come back to kill me. This is he, who has dragged himself out of the bowels of the earth to find me again.*

The hatchling climbs out of the bowl and lands, puddled, on the corner of the table. It stretches its feet down the table's leg with the utmost caution, only inching down further when its hind feet are properly situated. Still, when it jumps to the floor, it stumbles over itself. Droplets of water land at my feet.

"Where are you going?" I ask it, though it makes no move to reply to me. At my bedside, I fiddle with a charcoal stylus, chewing a hole through my parchment as I spin it faster.

I've spent my days pretending to prepare for my journey back to the monastery and dwelling on strange fantasies. When I see the map that I used to route my initial journey, I think instead that I might be swallowed up by the same muck that holds Diarseig and his brood. In my dreams, my mouth is full of dirt.

The hatchling's tail lashes; I think of the white serpent from the priest's book. Diarseig had a name, but this serpent does not. When I listen to the whispers of the townspeople, huddled in their market square, they speak of other creatures, too, which sleep below the ground and which guard their waters.

These same men, dogs at their side, watch the boundaries of their village with glinting eyes at nighttime, as if another dragon will emerge from its slumber and encroach.

The hatchling sits at the door, then draws its claws across the wood.

Such men would waste no time killing the hatchling as I had not hesitated in killing its father. The thought makes me nauseous, now, and I see the jelly of that single eye wrapped around my blade.

We leave in the cover of dusk, the hatchling coiled around my wrist. At my back, the sun sinks and lanterns glitter in windows. I duck beneath the tree branches; blackness falls over my shoulders. I walk until the stars form overhead, and I track my steps with their positions. When I can walk no further, I rest in the roots of a tree.

I know from their maps that there is a lake not far from here and deeper woods where the serpent may live—where I might return the hatchling to its cradle.

As I stroke its scales, it, too, sleeps. It has grown at a remarkable pace and now I can feel a swelling of muscle flanking its spine and see the shimmering stripes that line its sides. I wait for it to close its eyes.

It takes us three days to reach the lake. It stretches back until fog obscures the horizon. The land dips suddenly into swirling depths, so when I look down at the black waters, they look back at me with the same clarity as a mirror. Then, the waters split apart to reveal a single eye, molten copper and rolling beneath a scaled brow.

"There you are," this creature whispers. "I've been waiting for you."

My eyes widen and I wonder if it is speaking to me—but then the hatchling chirps and skips into the water. My fingers wrap around its tail right before it escapes me completely.

It looks back to me once before diving beneath the surface. I bite back a farewell and swallow its bitter taste.

The eye rolls to face me.

"They call me the White Lady," the creature in the lake says. "Those men who drink from me, though they have not seen me in years. Who are you?"

I think of my name. I think: a knight of the church. I think: a man.

"I don't know," I say.

The Lady raises his head from the lake. He cannot be more different from Diarseig. He looms above me, his delicate head perched atop a neck as long as I am tall. He is needle-like and shimmering white. I stumble backwards a single step before I find my resolve.

"You do. You are the man who has slain Diarseig."

"How do you--?" His words make my body run cold.

His mouth splits apart to reveal a stunningly red tongue. Strings of translucent algae hang from the sides of his jaw and shake. When he inhales, he sounds like the wind gusting. I think that he is laughing.

"You are stained with his blood!" the Lady says. "You think that you have washed yourself clean, but you have not."

The Lady brings his claws from the water and sets them on either side of me. I see them only in my periphery, shining like freshly polished steel. My heart quickens.

"I've returned to you his child," I say. "This is all I could save of his brood."

"Is this your repentance? After this, do you think that you will leave?"

I tighten my grip on the pommel of my sword until the engraved dove digs into my palm. I shift my foot backwards.

"Go on, knight-who-has-slain-Diarseig. Run."

Saliva drips from his jaw and onto my cheek. If I were to leave now, I know that his voice would follow at my heels, and then too, his claws.

"Did you love Diarseig?" I ask—too loudly, my voice tears at my throat. I wonder what sort of creature would dare weave between Diarseig's claws or prostrate itself beneath his stomach.

The Lady lowers his head until he is level with me. The dew dotting his forehead wets my skin.

"Diarseig is not his name." His breath brushes against my cheek. "It is the name of a mindless lizard who eats wolves. When I sleep in my lake, I hear the pulsing of the fishes' blood and the currents made when the ferns breathe; when I wake, I speak to them. So did he rule his kingdom and the trees whose roots burrow into my sands still.

"What an affront," he says to me, "to arrive here as his murderer. You should beg for your life."

With a slow hand, I wipe the drool from my cheek, and I breathe deeply enough to recover my voice. "Will it be safe here? The hatchling?"

He hums low in his throat.

I see at once the pink flesh of his throat and the iridescence of his teeth before he closes in on me, before his jaws crush the air from my lungs. I think that it should hurt. Both my blood and his saliva wet my clothes, then seep into the cracks of my skin. The sky blares above me, white, and there is sand at my back. On the waves, I see the shadow of the hatchling. I blink and this is gone, too.

LOREN'S CHOICE

N.R. WILLIAMS

Above the hearth was a collection of knives and in the center, Loren's fathers favorite, longer than the others with a polished walnut handle. All of them forged by her father and the envy of every household in the village of Navarife.

Loren sat down at the table and threw her long black braid over her shoulder. "Papa."

He looked up from leaning over his meal and set the spoon down from shoveling it all into his mouth. Her mother had her plate and sat opposite Loren with her back to the hearth.

"I want to be a blacksmith like you."

He grunted. "No girl." And resumed eating.

"But–."

"Listen to your father."

"He isn't talking." Loren frowned.

"You've been told, child," her mother admonished.

Her father set the spoon down, shoved his plate away and picked up the mug of ale. Downing it, he belched, wiped his mouth while slamming the jug on the table and then folded his fingers together.

"The gods didn't make a woman capable of learning

such a skill."

"How do you know?" She pushed aside her fallen lock that refused to stay braided.

"Mydisy came by." Her father let both his thumbs tap each other.

"What did he want?"

"Your hand in marriage." Visions of Mydisy's bulbous nose popped into her head. His father, the town butcher, was bald and already Mydisy had lost most of his hair.

Loren folded her arms. "No!"

"You will need to wed soon, daughter," he said.

Her mother nodded agreement.

To that, she began to list the eligible boys and her assessment of each. "Mydisy bobbing nose. Ziddi moist."

"The widow's son can't help that his hands sweat." Her mother gave her a stern frown.

Glancing at her mother she continued, "Gralla the buffoon, the horses try to kick him...often."

"He isn't a natural at grooming the animals like his father." Papa glanced at her mother as she stood to remove the dishes from the table.

"Nu-is run about."

"That will do." Her father stood. "Nuishe child, not Nu-is, he delivers goods for his father's store as you well know. All these young men are fine prospects."

"And if the emperor comes to town as you fear, Papa, they will all go off to the coming war. Then, I'd be a widow with a brat, and you'd have to take care of both of us."

"You listened to us last night?" Her mother stopped at the small work bench and set the dishes down.

"It's hard not to. You were shouting at papa."

Her father frowned and sat again. "It is a woman's duty to marry and bear children."

She groaned.

"Loren! Enough. Go fetch water from the well," her mother said.

She stood, lifting her chin as she gazed at her mother,

grabbed the bucket, and headed to the door. There she paused to hear her mother say, "See what comes from giving her your favor?"

Her father raised his voice. "If you see soldiers, run and hide."

Fear of the soldiers who sometimes rode through town was a palpable thing. The emperor sent them to kidnap girls as young as five and older. Loren had heard it so much that she ignored it now. Her thoughts returning to marriage.

I will never marry for duty. I want to love someone with passion!

Outside, the harsh sun made her squint. As she adjusted her vision a stranger rode by headed north through town. She stepped down from the wooden porch into the street and hurried after him. Master Sther and Dimrish, the butcher and store owner, stepped out of their businesses followed by their sons, Mydisy and Nuishe.

The stranger pulled his horse to a stop. Loren was close enough to hear what was said.

"What you be wanting?" Master Sther asked wiping his bloody hands on his apron.

The stranger leaned forward a little, peered at those gathered and spoke in the accent of those that had come from afar and were now threatening their emperor. Not that the emperor didn't deserve those threats. At least, Loren thought so.

"I have traveled a long way and would be glad of some food and drink."

"We don't coddle enemies," Sther said.

"Do you have money?" Master Dimrish asked glancing at Sther.

"Indeed," the stranger said and reached into his pocket.

"Come in, sir." Dimrish turned back into his store.

The stranger dismounted. He was taller than anyone in the village. His hair was just past his collar and light brown instead of black. He wore a leather jerkin, a sword at his hip and carried himself with his head high. *A nobleman?* But she wasn't certain and watched as he disappeared into the store.

The well was in the center of town and positioned off to the side between Master Sther and Dimrish's businesses. Mydisy and Nuishe had guessed her destination and both stood before the well watching her. She sighed and approached.

"Mistress Loren, may I help you?" Mydisy reached for her bucket, his hands bloody like his father's.

She stopped, pulled the bucket back behind her brown skirt and glared at him with what she hoped would be intimidation. "No."

"I will help her." Nuishe had circled around and grabbed her bucket before she could stop him.

"I'll draw the water." Mydisy began to crank. "After all, she is to be my wife." His eyes drilled into Nuishe.

"What?" Nuishe turned back toward her. "When?"

"I will not marry *My-dis-gore*," with emphasis on the last because of his bloody hands and apron. "No matter what he thinks."

"But your father–." Mydisy stopped cranking the water.

"Doesn't speak for me."

"Then, may I, for all I prize–."

"Oh stop, Nu-is. I won't marry either of you."

"Who then?" They said together.

"No one. Why should a woman have to marry?"

"Because she does," Mydisy said.

"What else could she do?" Nuishe asked.

"Let me see? Hmm…I could be a healer, a smithy---."

"You can't be a smithy." Nuishe gave her a once over.

"And why not?"

"You haven't the strength. Only a man can do such things," Mydisy pronounced.

"You're going to be the luhk of Navarife," Nuishe warned.

Loren noticed several of the towns people stopping to watch them and listen. Lypiva, the gossiping widow among them. She didn't care. Instead, she tossed her head away from Nuishe.

The stranger walked from the shop with several burlap bags. Loren turned to watch him. He glanced at her, smiled with lips that weren't too plump nor too thin. *Perfect lips.*

He turned aside toward his horse and tied the burlap bags to the saddle bags, then he mounted.

"Soldiers!" Someone yelled from behind Loren. They all turned back toward the south, even the young man on his horse turned the animal's head. Loren saw her father outside the forge. Far down the road, three men were galloping toward Navarife.

The men in town yelled, "Run home!"

Women cried and ran. Mydisy ran for the butcher's shop as did Nuishe. In minutes, the street was clear except for her father who was running toward her and the stranger.

"Come, girl." Her father grabbed her hand and began to run. He lost his grip and she faltered, looking toward the soldiers. They were closer but still far enough that they may not have noticed her.

An arm circled her waist and lifted. She grabbed at it. He pulled her across his lap, her legs dangling on one side and her hands on the other while her belly lay over his legs and saddle.

"No, stop!" Her father yelled.

The horse sprang into a gallop, through an alley opposite the well, out of the village, and into the meadow that surrounded the town. Her belly hit his saddle with every jolt.

Yelling above the loud beat of hooves she said, "What are you about?"

He didn't answer. The horse whip flipped against the animal's side and almost hit her.

"Ya!"

From a great distance she could still heard her father. "Stop!"

They reached the oak forest, and the man pulled the horse's reins. "Whoa." The gelding turned and danced a little to the side.

Loren hoisted herself off the horse, turned and ran back

the way they'd come.

A thud from behind.

"Papa!" His name splintered between her teeth as the stranger tackled her to the ground. Her hands slid on the grass. He turned her on her back and straddled her.

"What..." the word breathy from her efforts?

"Calm down."

She heard the bellow from her father, and something else. Horses at a full gallop. She tilted her head up and looked past the gap between several trees to see her father halfway there with the three soldiers advancing on him.

The stranger stood, pulled her up and ran her toward the horse. He mounted and reached for her hand.

"What are you doing?"

"Saving your life."

Without hesitating she gave him her hand. She sat on his lap this time straddling the horse. He kicked the gelding and they sped further into the woods. A fallen tree blocked their progress. The horse leapt over it and on they traveled.

The wind took her breath and she swallowed. They galloped for half an hour before he slowed his horse to a trot and continued their northeastern advance.

"Where are we going?" Loren scrutinized the woodland. Oak and pine, bushes, and wildflowers. She'd never been this far from home before and she had a sense of wild abandon. *Oh, how naughty. Alone with a man.*

"Away," he answered her question.

A short time later he slowed to a walk and they traveled on. Both silent. She listened for any sound of others in pursuit. After a while, she heard water rushing over rocks. The young man turned the horse's head toward it. He pulled to a stop, dismounted, and reached to help her down. Loren stamped her feet to bring sensation back into her legs and watched him lead the horse toward the water.

The small creek was full and lapped the sandy side. A slight incline led to the forest behind them. While the horse drank, he turned back to look at her.

"I'll catch some fish. You gather firewood." He began to lead the horse back toward the woods.

"Why?"

He stopped and turned toward her. His eyes amber with green flecks. She stood too close and backed up.

"We must eat, don't you think?"

"I mean, why should I not fish and you gather the firewood?"

A smile played at the corner of his mouth. "If you prefer."

The brown girdle that held her ribs and lifted her breast against the white linen blouse beneath it was way too tight making it hard to breathe. She smoothed her hands on her skirt, held her head high and marched past him toward the stream. Her father never took the time to travel to the creek and fish, preferring to buy fish from Master Dimrish. Because of this she'd never fished before and had no idea what to do.

He remained, the horse behind him. Loren stood at the creeks edge and studied the water. While full it didn't have a strong current. She could see a bed of rocks, and fish swimming back and forth. One rushed the surface to catch a fly. *Not hard at all.*

She sat and removed her shoes and then the long hose she had tied above her knee. Standing once more, she stepped into the water and caught her breath. It was cold and reached just above her ankles. She took several steps. The rocks were slippery, and she almost fell. Her wet skirt dragged, and the fish scurried around her. She glanced back and saw that he still watched.

"Go fetch firewood."

He didn't answer.

Loren looked up stream and to each side. Studying the area. Placing her feet apart with care she bent and put her hands in the stream. One fish darted toward her, she grabbed it, but it slipped through her fingers, then another and another. She released a breath and realized that she'd been holding it.

Bending again, she dipped her hands into the gentle pull of water. "Oops!" Rocking a little she righted herself and bent. A fish came close. This time she'd get it. Moving quick toward the aquatic life she grabbed, it wiggled through her hands and she fell, landing with a huge splash, her feet in the air, her shoulders low enough to get wet.

"Oh!"

Laughter. He was laughing at her. She sat and beat the water several times. "Scyrno, god of rivers, why do you mock me?"

Water splashing gave notice that *he* had arrived. His hand reached toward hers as his body blocked the sun.

"Let me help you."

She put wet hands in his dry ones, and he enveloped her fingers with his warmth. He yanked, she rose and found herself in his arms.

"Come." He turned and she felt his arm circle her, his hand at her waist. *Why did he have to be so handsome?*

At the shore, he left her, returning to his horse. She folded her arms and turned back toward the water. Now that she was drenched, her braid dripping water, and her body chilled, making her teeth chatter, she wanted to go home. He returned, fish net in hand.

She lifted her gaze to his. A smile tugged at her lips. Then she frowned.

"A net," he said.

"I can see."

He grinned and stepped to the water, entering it without removing his boots. He cast the net and pulled in three fish. Turning he said, "Do you want to clean the fish and cook or gather firewood?"

"I wouldn't have to gather wood if you hadn't been watching me."

"I didn't want you to get swept downstream."

"That hardly would have happened, the water isn't that high or fast."

"I found it…" his eyes traveled over her body. "Enjoyable."

"I'll get the wood." Loren turned, toward the woods, then stopped. *How could she forget her shoes?* Turning back, she sat beside them and began to lift her skirt. Her toes were clogged with sand.

He was watching. She frowned to let him know he'd better stop staring.

"I'll clean the fish." He left.

She grabbed the shoes and hose and went to the water's edge. Sitting, she washed her hands and feet and then struggled to put on the hose over wet limbs. Finished, she began her chore. Twigs and dry grass were everywhere which made it easy to collect them. When she'd gathered enough, she returned to their campsite.

The fish were spread out on a flat rock as he cleaned them. He glanced at her. Kneeling, Loren placed the wood on the ground.

"Put rocks around that," he said.

She did as he said.

When he finished cleaning the fish, he brought the stone over, cleared an area for it and set the rock in the middle of the wood. Then piled the twigs higher around the stone. He stood and went to the horse where he rummaged through the saddle bag.

"Does your horse have a name?"

"Fine Summer." He turned with a small box in his hands.

"And yours."

He stopped, crossed one arm over his middle, bowed and stood up. "Philippe Calimar, at your service."

She nodded.

"And you are?" Philippe asked.

"Loren Theattamish."

"A lovely name, Loren."

He knelt once more and struck the tinderbox to get a spark and light the fire. Loren left to collect a few more sticks, larger than those she'd already found. When she returned, she added what she had to the fire. The smell of the fish cooking made her stomach grumble. She sat close and watched as he served the fish on a wide leaf, one and a half each, and gave her a raw potato from one of the burlap bags tied to the saddle bag.

"Raw?"

He grinned. "Yes."

"You know you can cook them."

"Of course, but they take longer than the fish and I haven't a pot to boil them in water, so raw it is. I like them this way."

"You must be far hungrier than I, having gone without lunch. If you want the other half of this fish, you may have it."

"That is kind of you, thank you." He took it and sat.

"You are unlike any nobleman I've ever met." Loren pulled some of the fish away from the rest and ate.

He stopped eating to gaze across at her, resting one arm on his bent knee. "I? Why do you think I'm a nobleman?"

"Aren't you? The way you walk and hold your head up high."

He chuckled. "You aren't shy about holding your head high."

"If I hid my head under a cloak, I would have no respect from anyone. As it is, the women gossip about me and the young men fight over me. I am not so foolish to think they want me for me. My father is the blacksmith. They want a better price on his goods or to get them for free." She feared looking at him now, *what would he think?* When she did lift her gaze, he held the last of his fish without eating it. She took another bite of her own.

"Do you look at yourself in the mirror?"

"Every morning and at night to brush my hair." She took a bite of the potato.

"You are beautiful, Loren. The young men in town desire you because of that, not your father's goods."

A thrill flowed through her. *He thinks I'm pretty.* Lifting her eyes once more she found him sitting cross legged and drinking from his waterskin. He wiped the excess with the back of his hand.

"I'm not a nobleman. None of us are. However, our prince is. He comes from Swaisia, a land far from here across the great ocean."

"Why do you go to war with the emperor?"

"Because he is evil, a dark sorcerer giant who has kept all of you under a suffocating grip. We will free you."

"The emperor has been to war before and he has always won. For five hundred years."

"Do you know how he has lived so long?"

"He's a sorcerer. By magic."

Philippe shook his head. "By murder of innocence. He kills young women, drinks their blood and sometimes he even eats newborn children. It is said, he gains all the years of their life that he steals and adds it to his own."

Loren held the potato close to her mouth but now she couldn't eat. "My parents always told me to hide from his soldiers."

"Yes, and now with war pending, he has begun to do all of that more often."

She turned aside. Her stomach roiled. She took a breath, shut her eyes, and willed herself not to be sick.

When dinner was over, he tended to his horse, removing the saddle and reins, and brushing the animal down. As she watched him, she couldn't help but admire his care of the gelding, the soft words in a different tongue which he spoke to it. The horse nuzzled his chest and he laughed, petting its head.

Philippe Calimar, you are a kind man.

Loren woke. The fire burned low. Crickets chirped a song. Philippe stood talking with two small men. She closed her eyes to slits when he glanced her way. They spoke in a different tongue and she couldn't understand what they said. When the men had gone, Philippe laid down.

Sunlight woke her. Loren sat up and looked around. The fire was just embers and Philippe had vanished. But his horse was there. *Had she dreamt of the nighttime visit or was it real?*

She saw him, coming up from the stream with the net.

He grinned. "You're awake. Breakfast." He held up the net.

He'd let her sleep. If she'd been at home, her mother would have nagged her awake before the sun rose.

"I'll get more wood."

He plopped the fish down on a different cleaning stone and removed both of his waterskin straps over his head and off his shoulder setting them down.

Wood lay around the ground in every direction. When she returned, Philippe was still cleaning the fish. Five this time. She knelt and put the twigs first on the embers. They caught immediately. He brought the fish to the fire and retrieved an onion this time from the burlap bag, giving her one before taking a bite of his.

"You eat them raw?"

He nodded, "Saves time."

"Give me the knife."

He did and she first peeled her onion and then cut it. Once done she added it to the stone and the fish. Not long afterwards, both fish and onion were done.

"I think you'll like this better." She put both fish and caramelized onion on his leaf.

After eating several of the onions he said, "Excellent. Hate to tell you this. I know how to do that."

"Then, why don't you."

"I like raw vegetables and–,"

"It saves time."

He grinned and nodded.

When they had finished eating, he gave her one of the

waterskins. Loren drank and then put the fire out while he thrust his saddle over the horse. At the creek, she filled both waterskins and returned.

Philippe mounted and held out his hand to her.

"Where will we go?"

"Back. See if it's safe for you."

She gave him her hand. His arms reached around her holding the reins. She was safe.

He didn't gallop this time but walked his horse past trees and over pools of sunlight. Birds flew by, crisscrossing in their wild mating pursuit. Rabbits chased each other, between two trees she saw a doe and her fawn.

"I had a dream."

"What was it?" His voice smooth and deep. The accent made her smile.

"I dreamt two men came to visit last night and talked with you."

"That wasn't a dream."

She tilted her head to look up at him. A day's growth of whiskers spread over his chin and face.

Philippe gazed down at her with those amber eyes. "True, though not men, elves."

Loren tensed and pulled away to turn enough so she had a better view of him. "Elves?"

He nodded.

"But they are...they are...dangerous."

"Nay, we have an alliance with the elves to defeat Druas-Bradwr."

"An alliance?" Loren turned back, now a sense of dread filled her. Her gaze traveled to the top of the trees. Glancing from there to every bush, every stump, every animal that scurried away. Elves were known to hide from humans.

"Do not fear, they won't harm you."

Her entire life she'd been warned about the elves. "They kidnap children and those who are taken never return."

The horse continued to walk. The noises of the forest had grown ominous.

"Elves don't kidnap anyone. Druas-Bradwr does."

"They both do."

He said nothing further and remained silent.

They stopped beneath several apple trees. Their sweet-smelling flowers in full bloom. He dismounted behind her and then reached to help her down. There'd be no fish for lunch, the stream far to the east. He gave her another potato and offered the onion too, but she declined.

Back on the horse they rode until dusk chased away the sun.

"No fire this night. We are too close to your village."

"Why not continue until we reach it? Mama will cook a meal for us." Her stomach rumbled when she said it.

"Too dangerous to travel at night with no light, and if the enemy is in town, they will kill me and snatch you up. Need I say more?"

Between her fear of the elves, the emperor and an empty stomach, Loren couldn't sleep. She sat against a tree searching the darkness for any sign of danger. When her eyes began to droop, she fell over and slept on her side until Philippe woke her.

"I'm starving," she said.

"Another potato and an onion."

This time she took the onion and after a bite realized it wasn't so bad. A drink from the waterskin helped her to swallow it.

She sat before him on the horse once more.

They reached the oak forest outside her village and stopped. The urge to run home made her muscles tight. Philippe left the horse by some bushes and brought over a spy glass. He was quiet as he gazed toward the town.

"Take a look," he said passing the instrument to her.

Loren held it to her eyes. The soldiers of the emperor were everywhere. Her father stood outside his forge talking with several. Moving the line of sight, she saw all four of her suitors tied with rope and loaded into a wagon along with little twelve-year-old Llettin, Nuishe's sister.

Acid churned in her belly and bubbled up into her throat. "We must save them."

"We cannot. There are too many. But there are others along the road that watch for captured men and women. They will fight to free them."

She thrust the spy glass at him, lifted her skirt and began to run. She couldn't let them take Llettin to be murdered by Bradwr. Five more trees and then the meadow. Her heart burned with fear. He tackled her pulling her toward the ground. They rolled once and stopped. He lay beside her. His hands holding her arms.

She struggled. "I can't...can't let them take sweet Llettin." Tears formed in her eyes.

He pulled her closer. "Go now and you to will be taken to Bradwr."

She choked; her tears fell before a sob escaped her lips. Philippe cradled her head, ran his hand down her back and whispered in her ear. "We will kill the sorcerer giant Bradwr who would destroy all that is dear."

For a long time, she cried and then took a shuddering breath. Sitting, she pulled her legs up to her chest and hugged them. "How? With elfin arrows?" She turned her head to study him. He was a blur until she wiped the tears from her eyes.

"We have more than elfin arrows and more than their friendship. We have a trained army. We have a brave leader. We have Lysandra and her song." We have—."

"Wait. A song?"

"Yes, a voice with power that disturbs Bradwr's magic. He is being driven mad by it. Every time she sings, her power weakens the giant sorcerer."

Loren looked away shaking her head. "Do you know how ridiculous that sounds?" Her eyes met his with scorn.

"I have heard her sing. It is as if every dark thing is put asunder. As if my cares are lifted and chased away. We will prevail."

Loren shut her eyes and turned aside. The thought of

young Llettin being murdered by the emperor took root in her imagination and she couldn't so easily dismiss it. Standing, she moved away from him, back into the forest were the horse waited.

"Loren." He reached for her hand, but she snatched it away.

"Why?" She turned abruptly. "Why, can't we save her?"

"Did you count them?"

"No."

"I am but one man. There are more than thirty. If I try to save her, it would be suicide. And as I've said. There are others along the road, prepared to engage the enemy and rob them of those they have captured. We must trust in them."

Shutting her eyes once more, she remained frozen in place. The beating rhythm of her heart told her she yet lived. His hand circled her upper arm. Turning toward him, she felt the gentle tug of her chin to lift towards him. His hand cupped her cheek and sent fingers into her hair. His kiss, warm and persuasive made her surrender while her arms encircled his back. Desire flowed through her. Her body fit against his perfectly. She lifted one leg around his and he pressed her closer. His lips left her mouth to run along her neck and she gave a whispered sigh, running her fingers into his hair while her arms continued to hold his shoulders.

Philippe moved his lips to her ear. "I promise you." His whisper warm on her ear lobe. "We will defeat Bradwr and when we do, I will return and marry you."

The army had left Navarife hours ago, yet Philippe still waited. Loren looked his way often, touching her lips in memory. *How had she fallen in love with him? She didn't know him. And yet she had. In love to the depths of her soul, to her very core.*

Earlier, when he'd pulled away and left to disappear behind several trees, she'd shrunk in on herself. *Don't stop!*

But he had. She wanted what was forbidden. His reassurance wasn't enough. She knew they would lose to the giant emperor and then he'd die, and she'd never see him again. *Cruel life, she didn't want to live without him.*

Now, he came to stand beside her, his horse in tow. Mounting, he held out his hand and she once more sat before him on the horse. His body so close, warm, protective. His lips found the base of her neck and kissed her there. She shut her eyes and tilted her head. His mouth over hers. The horse began to walk.

"We cannot." He withdrew.

"Why not?"

"I would not soil you and leave you deserted should I be unable to return."

"All the more reason why I love you."

He smiled at that and kissed her forehead.

The town was quiet. No one was on the street. Still he eased his horse between two buildings and hesitated at the exit. Dismounting, he took the reins and peered around the buildings before at last stepping into the street.

Loren had never seen the village this empty during the day. Though it was close to supper, there were usually stragglers running last minute errands or wives drawing water. A sense of mourning hovered in the atmosphere. She wanted to see her parents, but a strange fear engulfed her. *Would they be angry that she'd run off with him?*

Her fear ended when her father stepped outside his shop and saw her. "Loren!" He bellowed. The sound seemed to shake the town. As he ran toward her, many emerged from their homes and businesses. Her mother ran toward them too. She let her father pull her off the horse.

"My Loren." His arms enveloped her body squeezing her face into his shoulder.

"My baby, my baby," her mother cried. Loren went to her as well.

When she broke away, her father was giving Philippe a once over.

"Papa, Mama, let me introduce Philippe Calimar, my savior and champion. An honorable man."

Philippe bowed.

Her father's expression cleared. He grabbed Philippe's hand. "My thanks, how might I repay you?"

Philippe smiled. "Wouldn't mind a little food."

"Dinner is almost done and there's plenty," her mother said.

"Come, come. Leave your horse with Master Edi."

Edi was the farrier. He took the reins from Philippe. "I will take good care of him."

Philippe nodded, glanced at Loren, and then walked beside her father back to their home.

Dinner was roast chicken with potatoes, carrots, baked bread, and butter. Philippe ate as if he'd never eaten before. After he finished his plate, her mother gave him another generous amount saying, "Nothing is too good for the man that saved our daughter."

Loren finished her plate in record time but declined more. After eating, she watched her father question Philippe about the coming war. Having heard it all before and fearful of the outcome, she helped her mother clean up.

Philippe spent the night on a pallet on the main floor while her parents retired to their room and Loren to hers. For a while she couldn't sleep, thinking of all that had come about. But at last, exhaustion took her into pleasant dreams which ended in a nightmare were Philippe met his end by Bradwr's own hand. The smell of frying eggs woke her, and she put on a clean shift before heading down the stairs.

"Come sit, daughter," her mother said presenting her with eggs, warm flat bread and milk. She found herself across from Philippe this time. Behind him was the hearth and above it she saw that all their beautiful knives were gone.

"The knives!"

"Bradwr's men took them. But I hid the prize knife and still have that one." Her father than turned to Philippe, stood, and left without saying anything. When he returned, he had the knife. Beautifully wrought with a sharp blade a little longer than most and the hilt was polished walnut.

"I want you to have it because of your care for Loren." He handed the knife to the young foreigner.

Philippe took it and studied the knife by holding it to his eye and sighting down the blade. "I will treasure this always, Master Theattamish." He nodded toward her father.

"Alas, I have lingered long enough, I must depart." Philippe stood.

"Let me wrap some food for your travels." Her mother turned and grabbed cheesecloth from a barrel.

Her father stood. "May the god of war, Nydara protect you."

Philippe hesitated, but if he wanted to correct her father he didn't. Loren knew he had his own god, though he hadn't spoken much of it on their travels.

He went to the door. Her parents followed and after a moment she too joined them.

"Here." Her mother handed him a loaf of bread, cheese, and jam while her father gave him a bottle of their best wine.

Loren caught Philippe's look, but her heart was so torn she couldn't move. He stepped down and crossed the street to the farrier's barn. Loren followed.

His horse had already been made ready and he gave master Edi a coin. He took a moment to put all her parent's gifts in his saddle bags and then led the horse toward the door where Loren waited.

She lifted her gaze to his. "Please don't go. No one will think badly of you." A tear escaped her eye and ran down to her chin.

He gazed at the ground for a long moment and then raised his eyes to hers.

"Papa can train you in the blacksmiths trade. I have no brother for him to pass it to."

"Loren." He took both her hands, letting the reins drop. "I have pledged an oath to serve my prince and fellows. I must go."

A shudder left her lips. "But I don't want you to die."

"I will live." He kissed both of her hands. "I will live, and return having defeated the evil emperor. Our children will grow up safe from such terror." He pulled her into an embrace and kissed her. Loren didn't care that the entire village was watching. She didn't care that some would accuse her of whoring herself to him. All she could think of was that she'd lose him forever.

He pulled away, rubbed the tears from her face and turned to mount his gelding. "I will return," he promised looking down at her and then he urged his horse into a trot heading north the same way Bradwr's men had gone.

She remained long after he had vanished. Her mother came at last to collect her and she cried the remainder of the day.

Spring gave way to summer. Loren did everything she could to forget Philippe Calimar. Yet, her mind strayed toward him, his smile, those eyes, the feel of his hair and most of all his kiss. At night she pressed the back of her hand to her lips and pretended it was him.

Since all the young men had been taken for Bradwr's war, including her father's apprentice, he'd relented and now she was his novice. The first couple of weeks left her so sore it was hard to pick up her spoon to eat. Her father rubbed his balm on her arms each night and after many nights the ache became a mild irritation. Now, after three months, her once thin arms were muscular. Not as much as her father's, but he was a man.

Sparks flew as she pounded the red-hot iron that would become a horseshoe when she had finished. She wore a leather apron over her shortened skirt that came to her ankles. The apron's top kept most of her linen blouse protected but the heat had persuaded her to remove the sleeves. Her long black hair was braided and then wrapped around her head and she wore a leather cap over it.

She thrust the finished horseshoe into the bucket of water and while it hissed steam, looked across at her father while lifting the eye patch from her left eye. A source of protection against the ever-flying red hot sparks.

"Papa."

He was working on a knife and paused to look up.

"I'm going for some water."

"Take care, child." He pounded once more.

He always said that. What did she need to be careful of? The town was deserted except for old people her parents' age and older.

The heat of July was still not as bad as the forge. She had two cups and a cloth with her. At the well she began to crank. No one came to help her. No young men to tease. She missed it.

When the bucket was at the top of the well and steady on the side, she dipped her cup in twice and drank. Then she filled both cups and set each aside. Last, she dipped the cloth in, wrung it out over the ground and used it to wipe her neck, face, and arms.

She shut her eyes and leaned back opening them again to look at the sun. The position of it told her it was just before the noon hour. Mama would be calling them into eat.

She let the well bucket drop back down, heard the splash, and put the cloth in the aprons pocket. Lifting both cups, she started back.

A tremendous boom shook the entire village and made Loren fall spilling the water. She sat and twisted back looking north. Far to the north lights still lit the cloudless sky. Closer was an invisible yet shimmering wall as high as the sky and outlined with sparks. The invisible wall traveled toward her at a rapid pace. There was no time to react as it hit her and pushed her down on her back. Her entire body tingled as it passed over her and then it was gone. When she sat and twisted, she could see it continuing to travel south, over the road and past the trees without harming them.

Every person in the village came out to watch it leave. Her parents were running toward her. They'd been so protective since her return.

"Loren!" Her father said.

"Are you alright?" Her mother's anxious voice quivered. She stood. "I'm fine."

"What was that?" Master Sther asked, Nuishe's father. He stood close, dark circles beneath his eyes told Loren he had trouble sleeping.

"I don't know. But my whole body prickled as it passed over me," she said.

Her mother patted the cap on her head and moved to her arms. "Come home now, lunch is ready."

No other odd thing happened after that. Weeks passed, the apple trees were ready to harvest and, on this day, they didn't work the forge, but set out with large baskets.

The townsfolk gathered in the street. After months of sorrow, it was the first time Loren saw anyone smile. Apple picking time made the close relationship of these people special. Even the busy bodies were friendly. Still for Loren, seeing no one her own age was a reminder that tragedy had befallen them and her thoughts once more strayed to the man she loved.

North of town, the road curved after a short distance away. Master Dimrish pointed and said, "Someone comes."

She turned, put a hand over her eyes to shield them from the sun's glare and looked. A lone rider traveled toward them, then a moment later a wagon turned the curve in the road and came into view, then another. Hope traveled through her and surrounded her heart. Lifting her skirt and dropping the basket, Loren began to run past those gathered. Past numerous buildings. Past open ground and then stopped. The rider was close now. The village people were coming as well. She knew him and a smile spread over her beautiful face as Philippe Calimar pulled the horse to a stop beside her.

He dismounted. "Loren."

She went to him, wrapping her arms over his shoulders. His kiss most welcome after the months of drought when she'd despaired. Pulling back, she saw the red jagged scar breaking one eyebrow in two.

"I told you I'd return."

"Yes, yes you did."

The wagons were close now and she saw many who had been taken. Pipho, Ziddi, Nuishe and his sister Llettin among them.

"Where is Mydisy?"

"He died fighting by my side against the emperor."

Now she regretted having been so cruel to him. "And the emperor? How is it he let you all go?"

Philippe smiled. "The sorcerer giant is dead."

Those in the wagon were now out and surrounded by family.

"The emperor dead?" Her father's question was joined by many of the villagers which made it sound like an echo.

"Praise be to God," Nuishe called out. "The emperor is dead!"

His arm around her waist, Loren walked back to the village with Philippe at her side. Joy radiated between them. Their love would reach new depths.

FOR NEEPA

A DAWN CLUSTER TALE

MARK J. SCHULTIS

THE PLANET POKTIQUE

This is it, Prock gazed at the shimmering acropolis behind them. *No turning back.*

As the sentrysled hovercraft descended through the fog, Prock and his Pochrill, his would-be commanding officer, were soon removed from the familiar royal grounds, entering a world hidden from all but the Verberus Guard. Not just the habitat of Poktique's animal life, the valleys below were also the refuse of all those exiled and banished by the lawagetas of House Libvi. The world of the unaesthetic. *I loathe such a vain and cruel practice,* Prock thought. *But that same practice has ensured Neepa's safety and happiness. That alone justifies it.*

And justifies my new commitment. The axitis. The hunt of admittance.

"Hear me well, runt," The Pochrill threw to Prock a Brahg Dagger, the blunt weapon of the Verberus Guard. A weapon Prock almost dropped. "I will not afford you any special custom," The Pochrill continued. "Lawagetas Celia requesting your axitis is her right, but no male with blood other than a Pokternian's can endure the tasks of the Verberus Guard. Why you've surrendered your life within the palace can only be understood with a fool's logic," The Pochrill leaned in close to Prock, his breath overpowering. "But heed my words. I stand down next season, and I refuse to leave behind a blemish on my service. Your breed cares not for honor. Better you accept failure today than die in disgrace."

Prock cleared his throat. "My only disgrace would be failure to try."

The Pochrill chuckled. "You have a set of rowers, runt. So be it." He slowed the sentrysled's descent, directing the small craft to a ridge halfway down the mountainside. "The first task of the Verberus Guard is to procure, to stock the kitchens of the palace. Hunting is in a Pokternian's spirit. What is in yours?"

"Servitude, which would include hunting if called for."

"Spoken like the house slave you are," The sentrysled landed and the Pochrill leapt out. "Down here, below the pampered life you've discarded, nature knows not of servitude. It only knows survival. Death. Predator and prey. What will you be?"

Prock clutched the Brahg Dagger with his coral fingers and climbed out of the sentrysled. "Predator."

"Very well. This ridge is ripe with fossti. Do you know of them?"

"Felines. Very delicious. We serve them for the Resting Day meal."

"Good. Bring one back to the sled or do not come back at all. Understood?"

Many of my peers called me daft, even suicidal. Perhaps one day love will inspire them as well.

Prock nodded to his Pochrill, then jogged along the ridge, following it until the terrain below his feet widened. The weeds and flora there had grown considerably, even several short trees had found a way to prosper on the mountain.

Fossti only stand as high as my knee... it'll be impossible to see any in this brush.

Prock waded into the growth, the cacophony of chirping insects so loud it masked the sound of anything else.

Nor will it be possible to hear one until it's on top of me. Perhaps I am daft to think myself Verberus Guard material. Composition, however, came naturally to me. Had it not, I would never have graced Neepa's presence!

As Prock slowed his advance, his mind wandered, reminiscing of the day last season when he was asked to perform his new musical arrangement for the royal family. He had never seen or heard the lawagetas or the princess, but the assessor he knew. Prock had met Assessor Sessia when he came of age. It was her role to estimate if his appearance and skill afforded him life within the palace walls. Prock's mother had chosen a Poktordian to sire him, so Prock not only inherited traits that lent themselves to intellectual pursuits, but fortunately his father had been a handsome one, and Sessia assigned Prock to the performing staff. As a child, Prock's mother not only instructed him in the politics of the Three Houses, but also in their art. She gave him a lute to foster his musical talents, and he spent years composing his own music, so within a short time of his assignment, Prock had already arranged a musical piece deemed worthy of royal audience. The audience comprised of Assessor Sessia, her sister Celia, who was the lawagetas, the queen of Poktique, as well as Celia's daughter, the princess Neepa. When Prock laid eyes on Neepa for the first time, he felt his heart skip a beat. Wrapped in a slender mint gown, Neepa's skin was the softest shade of pink, but unlike her mother, Neepa's naturally cyan hair had been dyed with sharp azure highlights. The colorful locks were draped over her neckline, the ends hovering above her bodice. And even with the lights dimmed, her eyes sparkled.

I was so distracted by her that I had tripped on my own pants leg while trying to get seated. Prock smiled. *Thankfully that amused her.*

Prock could still hear the performance in his head. The acoustics in the palace audience chamber were optimal, and he could not recall his music ever sounding as good as it did that day.

Perhaps my memory is biased by Neepa's smile throughout the performance?

Prock heard a rustling ahead, followed by a small rodent hopping onto the top of an overturned rock. It was cleaning its hands, while pausing to enjoy a ray of sunshine that had managed to punch through the fog above.

'Tis a universal truth that all life knows to enjoy the simple pleasu-

In a blur, a beast pounced upon the rodent and had it within its jaws. The rodent's blood dripping out of the feline's maw, the fosst cat turned its head.

And locked its eyes on Prock.

He is too small and too fast…

As the creature dropped its meal, Prock tightened his grip on the Brahg Dagger, swinging it as he backed up. A rock or some other outcropping was waiting for Prock's heel, and the former palace servant crashed to the ground, his dagger landing more than an arm's length away.

Radsi!

The fosst approaching, Prock reached for the blade anyways, desperate to arm himself. He didn't find the blade's handle but instead a sharp rock the size of a large fruit. He clutched it, and as the cat landed on his chest, Prock brought his weapon to its skull with all the force he had. The fosst let out a cry as it collapsed beside Prock, its hind legs twitching. Prock rolled over and found his blade. He bounced up onto his feet and stood over the wounded beast. Moments ago, it had tried to do to Prock what it had done to the rodent, and such is the way of things Prock figured. But the thought of taking its life gave him pause.

I am a stranger in this part of the world. Yet if not for the Verberus Guard coming down here, the families above would not eat.

Prock rotated the blade, the sharp end above the cat's belly.

For Neepa.

Minutes later, Prock returned to the Pochrill, dumping the fosst carcass in the back of the sentrysled. He wiped its blood off the blade and onto his pants leg.

The Pochrill was quiet a moment.

He did not expect me to succeed, Prock thought. *And yet I surprised us both.*

"The second task of the guard is to press, to use our strength wherever House Libvi needs it. The Verberus Guard will move mountains for the lawagetas if she asks."

"Yes, sir."

The Pochrill pointed to the mountainside. "Your return to the acropolis will be an ascent of your own hand." The elder man climbed into the sentrysled and turned on its engine. "Arrive by sundown, runt, or do not arrive at all."

With his eyes, Prock followed the mountainside up until it met the fog.

From that height, I doubt I would feel the impact…

The sentrysled lifted off, the air swirling beneath it as the craft quickly departed. It disappeared through the fog, leaving Prock alone to ponder his choice again.

Could I have spent another day off on the side as Neepa was courted by Poktordian businessmen? Could I have suffered another day of keeping our love secret?

Prock stepped forward.

For Neepa.

He spent several minutes accessing the mountainside where it met the ridge, looking for an area with enough footholds to make an ascent. Once he did, he took a deep breath and began his climb. With each reach of the hand, he grew more and more nauseous. He tried to keep his mind on his task, but on occasion found himself peering down, surveying his progress. When he neared the fog, the height he had reached became treacherous.

Focus. Mind and body. One goal. One purpose.

"What is my purpose here, my lady?" Prock had asked of Neepa two nights before. As they had done for several weeks, Neepa had called for Prock. 'To lull me to sleep with his soothing sounds' is how she put it to her mother when asked. The same story told to all within the palace as well. But the truth of the matter was in fact Neepa herself had grown just as enamored with Prock as he had with her.

Music had been his first love, but she had become the love that would define him.

"Your purpose is to love me, and I you." With her arm wrapped around his chest, Neepa had kissed his neck in response. "For as long as fate allows."

"Until you are asked to bear the child of a Hambrosi bureaucrat, or a Jerlosi savage."

"Libvi women do as we must to ensure out neutrality. But we do not wed."

"What if you wanted to though?"

"I doubt any off-worlder would ever woo me so."

"But a man of Poktique? Perhaps a musician?"

Her face had blushed, but the sadness in her eyes had nearly broken Prock's heart in two.

"Such a desire could never be justified to the lawagetas," Neepa had said. "But being with you is a desire that burns within me nightly. Fear not. Love me as you do, and I shall always seek you out."

"Unless your mother decrees otherwise."

"She would not! You are quite handsome, lover. I think she may be a tad jealous, even. Pray she does not call for you one night herself."

"What if I could justify it, my lady? To your mother? Prove myself worthy of your hand?"

"How so?"

"By joining the Verberus Guard. Demonstrating I have what it takes to protect you."

"Prock, where is your mind? They are savages from Poktern! They'll never accept you."

"You do not have faith in me."

"I have faith in your heart and your courage. But your mother chose a gentleman as your sire. Your hand excels at tenderness, not brutality. Or do you forget how you seduced me?"

"If I were in the Guard, I could be at your side within the palace and wherever you go. So, say you were to opt for holiday, a visit to Poktord? I would accompany you. And if you decided there was no need for us to return..."

"As long as House Hambrosi and House Jerlosi are at war, no one is taking a holiday. Now enough of this madness."

Prock had stared into her eyes, pleading her to listen. "Abandon your fear and listen with your heart. Would you have me at your side if it be possible?"

Her eyes no longer sad, Neepa had nodded, a tear running from her cheeks. "Yes, yes I would."

From there, they spoke about how to convince Celia to request Prock take the axitis. Neepa knew that it would eliminate any doubt Celia may still have had about their true intentions, but she also agreed with Prock that regardless of the outcome, it would prove his determination. They spent the night in each other arms, and Prock could still remember how her hair felt on his fingers.

The outcropping he gripped crumbled in his hand, and Prock quickly returned his attention and grasp to the previous hold. He listened as the falling pebbles clattered off the mountainside below.

Focus! You are no good to her splattered below on the ground.

Prock peeked down and saw nothing but fog.

Wherever that ground may be...

A powerful burst of wind swept through. Prock tensed up, his grip so tight he felt his fingers begin to bleed. Beads of sweat trickled down his salmon hued skin. He held his position until the wind passed. His arms shaking, he took a deep breath and resumed his climb. Battling an increased dizziness, Prock made his way up, penetrating the roof of the fog to see the top of the mountain finally within range. Reaching that height meant he also saw the sun, and that it had begun setting.

I must expediate.

One goal. One purpose.

With his last ounce of strength, Prock reached the top, hoisting himself up onto the grassy ridge to rest. He could smell in the air the floral bouquet of the acropolis gardens. He closed his eyes and inhaled, letting the scent calm his nerves. The breeze tickled his amber hair and Prock allowed his body to rest.

When Prock opened his eyes, his Pochrill was standing over him.

"With only moments to spare. Fate favors you, runt."

Prock lifted himself off the ground, his knees wobbling as he stood upright. "Yes, sir, it just may."

"Get yourself a meal. Replenish your energy for the final task and meet at the competitive circle after."

Prock nodded and watched as his commanding officer returned to the acropolis. Through a window above the Pochrill, Prock caught glimpse of Neepa. From behind the frosted glass his love waved. He returned the gesture.

I will be at your side. I promise.

Once Prock had helped himself to a supper of sparrow meat and berries, he indeed felt his strength return. He trekked across the palace grounds until he arrived at the competitive circle. All of the Verberus Guard were waiting, along with the royal family and their servants. As Neepa took her seat, Prock saw the anxiety she wore upon her face.

Fear did me no favors on the mountainside. I choose courage.

Since Prock was not of Pokternian descent, his frame was distinctively smaller than the rest of the Verberus Guard, so the armor he was offered was what once belonged to a former assessor, used for her recreational jousting. The chest and crouch pieces did not fit accordingly.

"If you walk away from this bout victorious, we will outfit you with new armor," The Pochrill handed Prock his sheathed weapon. "That is if you can walk away at all. The final task of the Guard is to protect. Our main purpose, the defense of House Libvi from any invaders. Once sworn into the Guard, you must be willing to give your life for them. Can you do this?"

Prock looked past the others and from afar met Neepa's gaze. Even in the black of night, her eyes still sparkled.

"Yes, I would give my life for them."

"Prove it," The Pochrill motioned for one of the Guard to join them. "This is Tralm. A cousin to Tsar Rilay Jerlosi himself. Best him and you will become one of the Verberus Guard."

Prock sized up his opponent. The Pokternian was almost twice Prock's size. His coral skin covered in armor much thicker than Prock's. *I must be crafty to succeed.* Prock nodded to the Pochrill. "Understood, sir."

The Pochrill pointed to the sheathed ends of the staff Prock held. "Blades are covered. This combat is not fatal, but your fighting style must be. This is the opportunity you foolishly sought. Prove your worth."

As the Pochrill and the others stepped outside of the circle, Prock and Tralm went to opposite ends until the lawagetas rang the bell. Prock felt the weight of the staff in his hands. *I do not have the arm strength for a crippling blow so only momentum can put enough force into an attack.*

Speed is the key.

Celia stood up; a small bell hung from her hand. "I now commence the final task of the axitis. Fare thee well, Prock."

The moment the bell was heard, Tralm lunged forward like a battering ram. Just as he bore down on Prock, the smaller combatant rolled to the side, evading his large opponent.

With any luck, I can tire him.

Prock ran for the other end of the circle, looking over

his shoulder to see his opponent gaining. Prock dropped to the sand, allowing the brute to overpass him.

On second thought, I may tire before he.

Tralm corrected his course and sprinted towards Prock. When his prey tried to duck this time, Tralm anticipated the move and followed, delivering a blow to Prock's ribs.

Almost dropping his staff, Prock crouched in pain, blind to the second blow. The force behind Tralm's attack sent him hurtling halfway across the circle.

His head woozy, Prock managed to return to his feet, taking note that Tralm hadn't moved yet.

He knows I cannot match him in strength and that he's proven it. Prock backed up to the opposite end of the circle, putting distance between the two. *He's playing with me, trying to humiliate me. Very well, then. Perhaps I should think of this as music. A crescendo is called for.*

Speed and momentum.

Prock propelled himself straight towards Tralm as fast as his legs could move. Tralm responded in kind, lunging forward. The two were on a collision course, but with his grip tight, Prock leaned himself back and to the left with the right end of his staff aligned with Tralm's chest. As Prock anticipated, with Tralm's mass what it was, the impact did nothing but recoil. Using that recoil, his footwork precise, Prock allowed the force of the recoil to pass through him, redirecting it into a spin attack with an upwards thrust that brought Prock about 360 degrees, and brought the right end of his weapon up directly to the back of Tralm's head.

When the movement came to an end, Tralm's helmet lie on the ground, his head exposed. If Prock's weapon hadn't been securely sheathed, the helmet on the ground would've been bloodied. The upswing would've slit the back of Tralm's neck, or with more force, severed Tralm's head from his body.

I think I won.

Celia, Neepa and Sessia stood and applauded, their servants joining in. The Verberus Guard remained stoic, although Prock could see the Pochrill grinning.

But Tralm was not amused. He did not believe it over. In a fit of anger, Tralm snapped his arm, extending it and his weapon with all his might. He made it clear his next move was of retaliation. But Tralm didn't see what Prock saw, what the onlookers had seen as well. When he snapped his arm, the force Tralm exuded to do so had dislodged the scabbard.

The blade end of his staff had become unsheathed.

Just as fast as Prock's movements had stunned Tralm, Tralm's movements came faster than Prock could properly react. Prock backed off a few steps before the lethal end of Tralm's weapon was at face level, enough steps to save his life. But the blade still made contact. The tip sliced across his cheek.

The pain Prock felt was not from the cut, but from upon hearing Neepa's shriek.

It… it is over now.

The Pochrill wedged himself between the two, pushing Tralm back before he could further injure Prock. Neepa's servants had rushed to Prock's aide, directing him inside to treat the wound.

It's all for naught.

The cut was deep enough. Prock could feel it. There would be a scar. His appearance would no longer be symmetric, his face no longer aesthetic in the eyes of the assessor or the lawagetas. He would suffer a fate worse than death…

I'll be removed from the palace. Removed from Neepa's presence.

Later that night, after the palace nurse had seen to his wound, Neepa paid him a visit.

Their last visit together.

"My love, you impressed many people today," Neepa sat beside him on the bed. "Defying expectations as you hoped to do."

"And by doing so, I had hoped to ensure my place at your side. Instead I've eliminated the possibility. Fate is malicious in its sense of irony."

"Your fear is premature," Neepa brushed her hand across his face. "The cut has not fully healed yet. And once it does, you'll still be the most dapper male I have ever lied eyes upon."

"You are blinded, my lady. Your aunt and mother are not. They will see the truth and make the call."

"Not if I persuade them to return you to the performing staff, and-"

"You can't persuade them. Not all of them. Tralm has been humiliated, bested by a palace servant. The Guard will not have me. They are his kin. If I stay, who knows what turmoil it may bring? It may rattle relations with Poktern."

"I am the princess of House Libvi. They'll do as I say."

Prock shook his head. "Was it not you, my love, who reminded me of the neutrality that must be kept? 'Do as we must' you said?"

Neepa's face erupted, the acceptance of her responsibility and Prock's fate hitting her all at once. "I cannot suffer to watch them exile you in disgrace."

"I accepted the challenge, stood my ground. There is no disgrace in that, my lady."

Her face powder smeared from the wiping away of tears, Neepa leaned in to kiss him. "You'll be my love, forever."

"And you mine, my lady."

Prock committed to memory every sense of their last embrace. The smell of her hair. The warmth of her body. The touch of her lips.

It would be the only memory that mattered.

As expected, within two days, once the nurse had confirmed the cut would leave a scar, Assessor Sessia decreed Prock unaesthetic. The Verberus Guard at her side, she led Prock out of the acropolis and to the sentrysled at the edge of the lawn. The Pochrill directed Prock into the craft and then powered it up. The sentrysled lifted off and banked toward the edge of the mountain top.

Before they descended through the fog, Prock looked

back at the palace, to the nearest window, and caught one last glimpse of Neepa from afar.

Goodbye, my lady. Perhaps one day fate will bring us together again.

As they descended further down towards the valley floor, passing the ridge where they had stopped days earlier, the Pochrill turned to Prock, handing him a Brahg Dagger. "Take this with you. You'll need it."

"But I'm not of the Guard."

"No, but you earned it, runt. For whatever that is worth to you."

Prock nodded, lowering the blade to his side. He looked over the side of the vessel to see a roof of trees below them.

The sentrysled landed in a clearing, and the Pochrill stepped aside. "Fare thee well, Prock."

Prock stepped over the side of the sentrysled, his feet snapping twigs as they hit ground. From within the trees he could hear bird calls, and that same chirping of insects from the ridge. Knot grew in his stomach. He turned to the Pochrill. "Are the others… are they still alive?"

"Many have been brought down here through the years. It is the way of things. But their fates were not of our concern. Surviving is a choice an exile must make for themselves. I suspect many did not. But you have something they didn't. Preparation," The Pochrill brought the sentrysled about and began his ascent. "Procure, press, protect. Tasks of survival. Remember them and survive."

Prock watched as the craft lifted off, eventually becoming a speck in the air, then vanishing all together.

This is it. No way back. Prock faced the mouth of the jungle. He raised his Brahg Dagger and took a deep breath, then took his first step forward.

Banishment is not death. Failure is not death. As long as she still breathes, so will I. I will survive. I will defy expectations. Theirs and mine. And I'll do it again and again.

For Neepa.

HE'S STILL WITH ME

BETHANY A. PERRY

I wake up.

I brush my teeth.

I get dressed.

The coffee brews. It's awful because I don't know how to make it like you did. It tastes like the bottom of an old shoe.

I drink it anyway.

I get in the car.

I go to work.

I smile at people. It's awful because the smile stretches my lips so tight, I can't feel them. I don't smile at them like I smiled at you.

I get back in the car.

I come home.

I cry.

That's it. Those are my days. My nights, well...

Those are a different story.

As the sun crept below the horizon, turning the sky into a riot of yellow, orange, and pink, Rose stared at the TV. She'd been flipping through the movies on some streaming app since she got home, staring blankly at each one. The tears had dried to her cheeks, leaving them stiff, and she hoped she wouldn't come across another of his favorite shows. That always set her off.

She glanced at his chair. Where he'd sit and watch TV, scroll his phone, and pay half attention to both. He always turned all his attention to her, though. Every time she spoke, he'd turn those large brown eyes on her and bat those deep black eyelashes and something in his face would lift. The corners of his eyes would lighten. He looked at her different than everything else.

Now that the sun was down, and the house ticked as it cooled, and the dark crawled through the windows and over the floor, she clicked the TV off and waited.

The dark crept through the room, stealing the light from the side table, from his chair, from her. Stealing it and taking it wherever light went when the night drew down like a curtain. A thick, red curtain like they used to use in theatres. The velvety color of blood.

Did the night caress her? Did it hold her in its dark arms until she fell asleep, still wearing his pajamas? She liked to think so. He had been taller than her, and his pajamas—worn thin at the crotch, the elbows, the knees—hung down almost like a dress on her. The pants bagged in the ass, flopping like an old flag ripped by the wind. But they still smelled just a bit like he did, and when the night embraced her, she thought she could smell him as he smelled now. His cologne the fresh scent of earth from his grave.

In her dreams, he truly came to life. In through the window, lying down in the bed as though he'd never left the slight depression from his warm body. Embracing her as the night had. They shared their bed again, every night in her dreams, and when she woke in the morning, weak, tired from the night, from pouring her love out to him as a pitcher of cool, clear water, she did the same thing she always did.

I wake up.

I brush my teeth.

I get dressed.

The coffee brews. It's awful because it's bitter and sour. Just like my life without you.

I drink it anyway.

I get in the car.

I go to work.

I smile at people. It's awful because the smile stretches my lips so tight, I can't feel them. All I can feel behind my smile is you.

I get back in the car.

I come home.

I cry.

That's it. That's another day. Another night, well...

That's a different story.

She turned off the TV and waited, like every night. But the dark didn't creep over her like it usually did, and after an hour staring at the shadows dancing on the wall in front of her, Rose got up and slid her jacket on over his oversized pajamas. She stuffed her car keys in one pocket and her ID in another and looked around for what she'd forgotten. Her mind as dark and blank as the wall she'd been staring at, whatever it was she was forgetting wouldn't come. All there was in her mind was that he was gone, that he hadn't come with the dark tonight, and something...she had to do something.

The radio in the car sat silent. She hadn't turned it on since his funeral procession. That drive from the funeral home, in the breath of daylight with her headlights on, and not stopping at red lights made her eyes jitter as she checked oncoming traffic. If they hadn't stopped, so much the better, but everyone pulled over and watched her pass, their eyes wide and hooded.

At this time of night, there were no other cars to watch from the spot her headlights carved out of the dark. No lights to change for oncoming traffic because there was no oncoming traffic. It was beyond the witching hour, and the streets were silent as the grave she'd watched his coffin lower into. An archaic thing, burying someone in a coffin, but she couldn't bring herself to let go of his body and so he rested there now, paint on his cheeks and lips, a suit that had been fitted before they slit it up the back resting on his sallow skin.

She stopped in the cemetery, far back from his headstone. It shone in the moon's glow, the silver light turning the grey marble bright white, the color of bone in the sun. On the passenger seat, a bouquet of red, red roses she bought a week ago. Every time she drove past the cemetery, going out of her way after work, she thought about delivering them to his grave. To leave them on the ground above his rotting corpse, an offering of blood and heart and suffering for the groundskeeper to throw in the trash once they had wilted.

But she hadn't, and now they sat in her seat, baked by the sun day after day, until they became what they were now—a mummified bouquet of spoiled love. She picked them up and the leaves crunched in her hand, the blossoms rubbing against each other, the petals whispering something only the ghost of a flower could understand. Her car sat running, the headlights shining as they had during the funeral procession, and she walked into the beams, her feet carrying her down the hill as though the only destination they ever had in mind was this one. Nowhere else would they carry her but back to him.

She knelt, laying the crunching bouquet on the corner of the headstone. The turned earth still fresh under her knees, spongy and wet, she sat in it and stared at the words on the stone. It had been delivered quickly, almost as though the engraver had been awaiting the order, with the name and dates chiseled and ready. The headlights from her car still shone, shadows deep inside the letters on the grave, each piece of his name only half what it was, shrouded in dark on one side and blinding white on the other.

Her hair glowed, the lights hitting her head now that she sat, the thick, muddy earth soaking into his pajamas. Erasing the scent of his life and stamping the odor of the grave into them, for now and for all.

At least, when he did come to visit her, she would only smell his new scent, now.

I wake up.

I brush my teeth.

I get dressed.

The coffee brews. It's awful because it doesn't taste the same. Even the air tastes a bit like poison.

I breathe in anyway.

I get in the car.

I go to work.

I smile at people. They don't smile back. They can feel you on me. They can see you in my eyes and they look away.

I get back in the car.

I come home.

I cry.

That's it. That's my life now. Your life? Well...

That's a different story.

It started the same way it ended. Cold, and bloody. There'd been no explanation from the doctors why he was in the condition he was. He walked home from work every day, feet pounding the concrete sidewalks each evening as the sun set ahead of him. In the winter, it went down faster, and by the time she saw him coming down their street, he disappeared into the dark between puddles of light rained down by the streetlamps, always reappearing in the next cone of artificial sun.

The night, that night, when the lamps held the dark at bay with their light puddles, he never reappeared. He simply walked into the dark between the lights and vanished. She couldn't run to find him, see where he was hiding, because the dark that swallowed him choked her, clogged her throat, covered her heart in a fear so deep it was like a trance. A wide-eyed, cold, suffocating meditation that blanketed everything in the dark of night.

Had she really ever left that darkness?

When the kids doing road clean-up, nothing more than nine-year-olds picking up the garbage people discard from their windows like the confetti of a disease, found him by the side of a street a hundred miles away, he was ripped apart and cold. So cold. Blood surrounded him, the grass beneath him the color of rust, the blades stiff with it. But his face, his face had still been perfect when she saw him lying in the morgue, calm and serene under his sheet. How could she destroy his face in flames? How could she allow the mortician to fill his body with fluids that smelled like eighth-grade science class nightmares?

They put makeup on him in the casket. So thick, the pores of his skin didn't exist. The darkness that had taken him—enclosed, engulfed, become him—couldn't escape him there, it had to hide under layers and layers of paint made to make him look alive. Made to comfort her in a world where his arms no longer could. And when they lowered the closed casket into the ground, she waited until the dirt covered it in that same darkness. The dark that had swallowed him before her eyes.

I wake up.

I brush my teeth.

I get dressed.

The coffee brews. I don't drink it. What do I need from coffee when I don't have you?

I breathe in.

I get in the car.

I don't go to work.

They fired me after a month of this. Once they heard about the exhumation, they backed away with wide eyes and grimaces.

They don't understand.

I have to see you.

To see you still in the ground.

Still in the dark.

Standing beside the ragged, overturned grave—the grimace on the face of the gravedigger as he did his job in reverse hurt her own mouth in its severity—she chewed every single fingernail down to the quick. Until the red blood beaded along the edge of her destroyed nails, until the pain of exposed skin burned all the way to her palms. And still the hole spat out reddish-black earth, clay loam lying in lumps on the green grass beside it. Waiting, sucking the blood off each of her fingers in turn, she tried to breathe but could only find the breath that'd been stolen from him. Stolen from him between the puddled light of one streetlamp and the next.

The grumbling backhoe stopped, dumping one last load of earth onto the pile of soil standing naked next to the hole he was buried in. One man jumped into the hole with a shovel and another joined him, and they worked without words, only the sound of their shovels scraping through the dirt and the steady *thump, thump, thump,* of more pieces of the ground meeting the sunlight once again when they flopped to the top of the pile breaking the silence. Once, one of them sprayed her with a shovelful, chunks of it landing and sticking in her hair, but Rose didn't bother telling them.

Instead, she stood and watched, eyes wide, pieces of his grave clinging to her hair, her breast, the lapel of his second-favorite flannel shirt. She stuck another finger in her mouth, pulling the blood off the nail with the tip of her tongue, the raw end between her teeth.

The shovels stopped scraping soil and hit wood.

The casket she'd buried him in. Still intact.

More machinery crunched through the graveyard, rolling across the resting places of others, packing the earth onto them so tightly they would never be able to dig themselves out. The crane stopped and waited as the men attached ropes to the coffin. And then it pulled the box out for everyone to see.

The clay had stained it red. Red on every surface, red dripping from the bottom and falling to the ground in clumps. Red the color of rust, red the color of old blood. Red the color of the slashes on his body that never had time to begin to heal.

The coffin next to the open grave, they pried it open and stepped back.

Still in repose, hands crossed on his stomach, his naked face stared up into the sky and his lips... His lips were red, red as the roses when she bought them, red as their satin petals.

She sank down to the ground next to him and stared into his face, wondering at how perfect it still was even after weeks underground. The mortician had admonished her, "the flesh will decay quickly without embalming, you must bury him before week's end," and she had. Yet, here was his flesh, soft and supple as the day he died.

They took his coffin away, back to the refrigerator so that she could transfer him to what she had called a "private cemetery," and she sat and stared at his tombstone. He had been in the ground all along; he had been in the cold grave alone where she left him. But now he was out of the dark and into the light and she would never banish him to that place again. It had been wrong to lay him under the ground. He would come home with her once more and wear his favorite pajamas and make love with the lights on.

Long after sunset she waited, watching the streetlamps illuminate one by one by one. Watching them cast their pools of light, beating away the dark, and waiting. Waiting for him to walk out of the dark and into the light.

And he did.

Rose gasped aloud when he walked into that next cone of orange light, a smile on his red, red lips and a spring in his step. Still wearing the suit they'd split up the back, the jacket flapping against the back of his arms. Her eyes wide, she could only watch as the front door creaked open and he stepped over the threshold, home at last. And when he pulled her into his embrace once more, a moment the size of a baby's breath passed before she knew what had happened to him when he disappeared into the dark. He pulled her into it with him now, his red lips against her throat, a stinging cold stippling her neck in gooseflesh, before the warm blood from her own artery gushed down the side of her body, staining his pajamas in the same red of his lips.

The red of fresh blood, pumped from the heart that beat only for him.

She closed her eyes.

I wake up.

EVEN THESE DECISIONS

R. A. MEENAN

Ryuichi Omnir approached his fixer-upper home after a long day of work at the hydro-electric plant, his red fur soaked with sweat. Draso's horns, he felt like shit. Fifty years at the same job and it never got any easier.

Didn't help that he came home to an empty nest now. His grandchildren, grown and gone off to start their adult lives. His son, killed by a madman. His wife, vanished and probably dead trying to go after that madman.

All that he had left of her was the Gem at his side. He absently stroked the belt pouch that held it, mentally calling on its power.

He shook his head, his red quills rustling, and dropped his hand. Best to let go of the dead. He just needed a long, hot shower. He opened the front door.

Solas' hologram sparkled into life the moment he

stepped in. The red and gold Chinese dragon peaked around the corner of the living room wall, her felted ears flat against her head and her expression somber. Her hologram flickered, a sure sign that she was tense.

Ryuichi flicked a catlike ear back. That wasn't good. "What happened?"

"You'll want to see for yourself, I think," Solas said, the A.I.'s voice shaking slightly. She fiddled with her clawed hands. "Or hear, really."

"I've had a long day, Solas," Ryuichi said as patiently as possible. "I don't have the mental capacity to listen to your strange radio waves from space. I'm sorry that you're bored here, and most days I'm happy to listen, but damn it, I need a shower."

"Ryuichi," the dragon said, betraying an unusual seriousness. "Trust me. You need to hear this." She disappeared around the corner with her drone holoprojector.

He sighed. Okay. Humor the bored A.I. for a moment, then go take a shower. He could do that. Begrudgingly he headed for the office.

Ryuichi leaned back in his battered office chair, fiddling with a pencil, refusing to believe what he just heard. And yet... "Play it again, Solas."

Solas flicked back a felted doe ear and twitched a long whisker. Her image flickered again. "Are you sure?"

"Just play it, damnit."

Solas affected a shrug with her short arms and manifested a large pearl. It glowed while the message played.

"*Are you mated?*" a dull bureaucratic voice droned.

"*I'm married,*" responded a feminine voice.

Ryuichi winced. There was just *no way...*

"*Livestock can't marry,*" the bureaucratic voice continued, unperturbed. "*Does your mate have a name?*"

"*Livestock!*" the first voice responded. "*Are you serious? Is that how you see people below your stature here? You uppity, heartless little--*"

"*If you are mated, give me your mate's name, or we will find a mate for you.*"

A pause. Ryuichi's fur and quills stood on end.

The feminine voice responded. "*Ryuichi Omnir.*"

The name hit like a punch to the gut. Damn it all. *Damn it all!*

Solas' pearl stopped glowing as the recording ended. She waved a hand and it vanished in a burst of colored sparks. She stared at Ryuichi with one emerald eye. "There's no mistaking it, Ryuichi." The dragon coiled up on Ryuichi's desk, her hologram flickering slightly as she processed the information. "That's your wife I picked up. That's Solana."

Ryuichi ran a hand down his red face, his fingerclaws catching little tangles in his fur. He flexed his hand and resheathed the claws, fighting agitation. Why did this have to happen now? He shook his head, his quills bristling.

His wife was supposed to be dead. Murdered by that madman Theron last year. He had come to terms with that. She was *dead*. He was done mourning.

And now here was Solas, with her voice on a recording that the dragon literally plucked out of the darkness of space. Damn her boredom-induced hobbies.

Solas "sat" patiently on the edge of the desk, flicking her feathered tail and stretching her wings. She ran long claws over one of her antlers, as if to sharpen it. Her drone holoprojector hovered and hummed like a ghost, bathing Ryuichi's dark office in a faint, ghastly glow.

The dragon A.I. had been an unwitting gift from Dyne Gildspine after the Sol genocide took Dyne's life. Ryuichi kept her to honor the friends he had lost in that tragedy.

For the first time ever, he regretted that decision.

"She's supposed to be dead, Solas," Ryuichi said. "Why the hell is she alive? *How* the hell is she alive?" He flattened an ear. "You're sure this is recent?"

"The file was dated," Solas said.

"You said the file came from a *different planet*," Ryuichi countered. "Why is it dated with Earth dates?"

"It's not," Solas said. "But it's from a planet I know. According to the conversion charts, this is two days old."

Two days. Draso's *mercy*. "How the hell did she end up on a different planet?"

Solas shrugged. "Your guess is as good as mine."

"Hypothesize."

"She had one of the Gems when Theron attacked her," Solas said. "If you remember, he hit the Gem when he threw that knife."

Ryuichi shuddered. He did *not* need the reminder. "The Gem exploded. We both saw the crater. There wasn't even anything left."

"Assuming that's what happened."

Ryuichi lifted a brow, perking his ears. "What else could it have done? You said it yourself. Damaged Gems release all their magic at once. It destroys everything in its path."

Solas looked off, twitching her felted nose. "Well... in theory..."

Ryuichi narrowed his eyes. "Spit it out, Solas."

"She might have teleported," the A.I. said, her voice going quiet.

"Teleported." Ryuichi raised both eyebrows now. "Can Gems do that?"

"Not these days," Solas said. "But there's historical evidence that they used to be able to. The Sol Gems were quite old – left over from the colonization from Zyearth. It could have easily had that power at one point. What if it teleported her when it released its magic?"

"To another *planet*?"

"Stranger things have happened."

Ryuichi stared at the floor, chewing his lip. "But why do they speak English?"

"Most planets do, at least some form of it," Solas said.

"Zyearth made the language popular with the colonization. Where do you think *your* planet got it?"

Ryuichi snorted. "England, perhaps?"

"They just adopted the word," Solas said, flicking her tail. "I know you're trying to find a way out of this, Ryuichi, and I won't let you. This is real, whether you accept it or not."

He squeezed his eyes shut a moment, then glanced at Solas. "So what do I do with this information?"

Solas tilted her head, her golden antlers catching sunlight. "Go after her?"

"How?" Ryuichi said. "There aren't any space planes on Earth that can do that except for--"

"Dyne's X-Zero."

"--Which I don't have the Gem shards to power and the plane hasn't been used in nearly fifty years."

"That might matter for one of Earth's commercial planes, but not a Zyearth space plane," Solas said. "A space plane that won't function after sitting for fifty years doesn't do much good to a population that lives four hundred years. Get me in there and I'll get it flight-worthy."

"Not without Gem shards, you won't," Ryuichi said. "I won't have the power."

Solas lowered her emerald gaze. "You're Black Bound."

Ryuichi bit his lip and glanced at the blood red Gem that now sat on a wire stand at the edge of his desk. Nearly the size of his fist, he had picked up the Gem on the island of Sol.

It was the very thing that drove his tribe to attack Sol in the first place nearly fifty years ago. He had hoped that by pilfering one of the Gems and bringing it to his brother Kyo, who headed the tribe, he could convince him not to attack.

But he didn't want just one Gem. He wanted them *all*. And he was willing to destroy all of Sol and even his own people to get them. The massacre left nothing behind. Full genocide of both Sol's people and his own people.

Except Ryuichi and his wife.

Ryuichi had fought Kyo, and in the battle, the Gem had reacted, and he bound himself to it. He only learned later from Solas that the Zyearthlings called that Black Binding. A rare bind that most Zyearthlings feared.

But it did make him extra powerful. Maybe he could power the plane.

"What if that doesn't work?"

"We could try the unbound Gem," Solas said. "I'm pretty sure the X-Zero had a slot for that. It might make up for the missing Gem shards."

"Might."

"You won't know until you try," Solas said. "We should check it out."

Ryuichi sighed. "…Okay, you win. Let's head over to Sol."

"I hate this," Ryuichi said. He stood barefoot on a beach near the old casinos, staring out over the dark sea that lay between him and the Trinity Islands. The dawn barely transformed the black sky to marine blue, painting a subtle outline of the islands. Sol, the middle island, held Dyne's X-Zero.

He flexed his toes, forcing sand between unsheathed claws. He hadn't been to the island since the genocide.

Solas' drone projector popped out of the pocket data shard holder and the dragon A.I. appeared above Ryuichi's head. "I know it's not pleasant, but we've got to try, right?"

"It's not just visiting the island," Ryuichi said. "It's *everything*. The islands, the plane, the situation… her voice…" He patted the cloth pouch that held his Gem. "The Gem. Everything." He held up a hand and called on the Gem's magic. Tiny globs of water formed around his palms and floated about like fairies, reflecting the little light from Solas' projection. "Even the magic."

"If it wasn't for the magic, you wouldn't be able to even get to the island."

"Which is a curse in itself," Ryuichi spat. "Let's just get this over with." He made sure Solas' data shard was snug in its waterproof pouch, then stepped out into the dark waves. His Gem whined slightly as he pulled the sea around his legs up to his waist, until it held him firmly in a slow-moving waterspout.

Then he held his hand forward and silently commanded the water to carry him toward the island.

Twenty minutes later, he hit Sol's shore. He dropped to the sand, breathing heavily, and used his magic to flick away water. Draso's horns, that was such an energy drain. The Gem's whine faded after he brushed the last of the water off his fur.

Solas floated above his head, her brow furrowed. "We made it."

"Still not sure that's a good thing," Ryuichi said.

The sun had edged over the water now, and though the beach was still shaded, the faint light meant Ryuichi wouldn't be searching in the dark.

He stood and glanced around. Forest and brush grew wildly out of control since no one inhabited the island anymore. While he was grateful for the ecological protections keeping it from being developed, he also didn't like the prospect of facing Sol's ghosts in the overgrown forest.

"Got an idea of where the plane might be?"

"Dyne hid it on the other side of the island."

"Of course," Ryuichi said. "Let's get started." He trudged through the underbrush, purposefully avoiding any trails. The last thing he wanted to see was any of the remains from the genocide victims, no matter how decomposed and unrecognizable they might be.

The ghostly huts still haunted him through the trees, however.

When he caught sight of the central square and Sanctum on his left, he knew he was headed in the right direction. Another ten minutes around the Sanctum and he entered the wild woods where Dyne supposedly left his plane.

Solas floated about his head, scanning around, looking for any sign of the Zyearthling technology. She stopped in midair, pointing a claw. "There."

In a small clearing, covered in dust and forest debris, stood the plane. Deceptively small for the room inside, it definitely carried the air of a space plane – swooping back wings, dark, foreign metal, precious few windows, and the ever-present Defender symbol plastered everywhere. The legless, winged dragon supposedly symbolized peace, though Ryuichi never associated dragons with anything peaceful.

Solas hovered over to the door and pressed a claw to a panel next to it. The door opened without fanfare, spraying dust everywhere. Solas met Ryuichi's eyes.

Ryuichi bent an ear back, his short tail sagging. He stepped into the plane.

There interior was, surprisingly, almost dust free, though everything smelled stale and metallic. Solas flipped on a light on her drone, scattering a few bugs, but it was well maintained.

Maybe this thing could fly.

"This way to the bridge," Solas said, floating down one hallway. "Let's see what your Gem can do."

It was a long, quiet, dark walk to the bridge. Ryuichi kept his gaze on Solas, trying to ignore the echoes in the halls.

Dyne used this plane. And he died on this island. Damn it all, he hated this.

Eventually the dragon stopped. "We're here."

The bridge was deceptively simplistic. Two chairs at a panel of instruments with comfortable benches behind them on one side and a series of chairs with straps on the other. There was a window at the front, though a black screen covered it now. Everything had a thin layer of dust and smelled of grime and musk.

Ryuichi brushed the seat of the captain's chair, sat down, and pulled his Gem from its pouch on his belt. Solas highlighted the Gem chamber.

Ryuichi stared at it. "I don't want to do this."

Solas twisted about in the air, her whiskers drooping. She dimmed her light. "You don't want to save your wife?"

Draso's horns, that made him seem monstrous. But how could he put everything into words? How could he make Solas understand? Ryuichi sat back in the chair. "Just… give me a minute. Maybe go check out the rest of the ship."

Solas flicked her ears back but nodded and exited the chamber. The only light left came from Ryuichi's Gem and Solas' data crystal.

Draso's mercy, what the hell was he doing here? Chasing the ghost of his wife, surrounded by the ghosts of his friends? Immersing himself in the sins of his past? He had no right to be here. No right to contemplate taking Dyne's ship, a friend who died because Ryuichi was too weak to stop his murderous brother.

He had already lost everything. And he deserved it.

Damn it all.

He should just leave. The Gem felt heavy in his hand. He moved to stand.

But his wife's voice echoed in his mind. Behind that firm, no-nonsense attitude, a faint hint of fear. He never knew her to fear anything. Not even the Omnirs during the genocide. Not Theron as he hunted their son.

So what scared her?

Damn it all, why was he considering this? Assuming the plane was space worthy, assuming he could get to this other planet, assuming he could *find* her, assuming she wasn't *dead…*

What the *hell* was he *thinking?*

That tiny hint of fear…

Damn it.

He flipped open the door to the Gem chamber, dropped

the Gem in it, then activated the power converter.

The plane immediately lit up, humming and creaking like an old water heater. The instrument panel beeped and buzzed, displaying a hundred tiny readings that meant absolutely nothing to Ryuichi. The dust on the panel warmed with the electronics, giving everything a haunted, dark smell that Ryuichi couldn't name.

Damn the Zyearthlings and their technology.

"Hey, you got it working!" Solas floated overhead. She examined the instrument panel. "Readings look good, too. I'll have to run diagnostics, but these are promising. Drop me in the A.I. slot. We could get this flying in no time!"

"Lovely," Ryuichi said, sitting back. He reached for Solas' data crystal.

And his phone rang.

Solas checked the call through her silver pearl, then curled into a ball. "It's... Trecheon."

Shit. *Shit.* "Is he on his cell or is he calling from the base?"

"His cell."

Damn it all! "Put it through." Solas lit up the pearl and connected the call. Ryuichi took a deep breath. "Hi, Trecheon."

"Hey Granddad!" Trecheon said, his voice unusually cheery. "Ryota and I got permission for an early leave. We're hoping to get to the station at the same time Ayumi does and surprise her. You sure you have space for all of us?"

Ryuichi shut his eyes tight. With everything going on, he forgot the family had planned to spend time together over the weekend. Their last hurrah before Trecheon and Ryota finished boot and got shipped off and Ayumi started college proper.

Shit. Going after his wife would mean leaving the kids behind.

And that would leave them vulnerable to Theron. The same madman who killed their father when they were little. The same bastard who tried to kill his wife. The asshole bent on trying to use the Omnir family for grandiose plans Ryuichi couldn't even begin to understand.

Putting Ayumi through college and encouraging Ryota and Trecheon to enlist were the only ways he knew to protect them from the enemy they knew nothing about. Get them far away from here, hide them in places where he'd never find them.

Hell, that was half the reason he even kept the bloodied Gems from Sol. He couldn't save his son, but damn if he would let that asshole get his grandkids. If he had to use the Gems to do that, he would.

And it's not like Ryuichi could tell them anything. Imagine trying to explain to them that some insane murderer was bent on using them simply because of their last name. They'd have him committed.

But if he left, they'd have no one to protect them.

"Granddad?"

"Sorry," Ryuichi said. "I'm kind of out of cell range and you're coming in choppy. Don't worry though, I'll find space for you all. It's just one weekend."

"Awesome," Trecheon said. "I'm looking forward to it!"

"Yeah… same," Ryuichi said. "See you all tomorrow." He hung up the phone.

Solas didn't uncurl. She blinked at Ryuichi with sad eyes.

Ryuichi rubbed his temple. "What do I do?"

Solas slightly uncurled, twitching her long whiskers. "You could just tell them."

Ryuichi rolled his eyes. "Yeah, that'd work. 'Hey kids, I know I've kept this from you your whole lives, but I actually have a super advanced dragon A.I. that my friend from another planet left me after your granduncle murdered him and his entire tribe in cold blood, trying to get these magic Gems that grant extra-long life and superpowers. She picked up a recording of your dead grandma talking about livestock on a different planet. I'ma take a fifty-year-old spaceship, leave you all behind, and go find her, okay?'" He shook his head. "Either they'd die from shock or they'd put me in a home."

Solas shrugged. "They're adults. They can take care of themselves."

"Under normal circumstances, maybe," Ryuichi said. "But Theron…"

Solas' image flickered. "You may have a point."

"I *do* have a point," Ryuichi said. "As long as they're off doing their things, and I'm here keeping Theron guessing, they're safe. But if I leave, how can I guarantee their safety? It's not like I'm just popping in and out for milk. I don't know when I'll get back. *If* I get back. If I even *get there*. And even if I get back, how many years will it be? I have four hundred years to live now – my grandchildren don't." He buried his face in his hands. "Damn this whole situation. And damn you too, Solas."

Solas frowned, and her avatar vanished.

Ryuichi pressed his lips together. Maybe it wasn't really fair to blame Solas. But damn it, this was not a decision anyone should ever have to make.

He plucked Solas' drone out of the air, ejected his Gem, and headed for home.

The trip back was uneventful. He got a decent night's sleep, managed to get to the kids from the station on time the next morning, and had a reasonably pleasant dinner that night. His grandsons regaled him with stories from boot camp. Trecheon, the more practical of the two, focused on the positive – his skill with a firearm, his prowess at hand-to-hand, his new friends, including a puma named Neil who Trecheon described as a "jackass-on-a-stick" but still good company.

Ryota, ever the fatalist, focused only on the negative. Ryuichi didn't encourage it.

Ayumi talked excitedly about her new dorm and the

friends she had made during her first week. Apparently, her work study job would be working in a costume shop on campus and she couldn't wait to get started.

After dinner the kids watched a movie and Ryuichi sat on the patio with a drink. Good Draso, what the hell was he supposed to do? Stay here and keep protecting his grandkids? Or risk everything and go search for his wife? No answer was right.

Damn Solas for finding that recording.

"Hey, Granddad?"

Ryuichi turned. Trecheon walked out on the patio, holding an open beer, frowning. He pasted a red, black-tipped ear back and his quills rustled in the light breeze.

Ryuichi narrowed his eyes. "You're not old enough for that yet."

Trecheon scoffed and took a swig. "Like that matters in boot."

"It matters in my house," Ryuichi said. "Dump it out."

"Killjoy," Trecheon said. He poured the rest out in a bush, then sat down. "I noticed you're not watching the movie."

"I've got a lot on my mind."

"Regretting the empty nest?"

Ryuichi snorted. "Hell no. I'll be glad to have your asses out of here."

"Ha!" Trecheon picked at a loose thread on his pants. "...Grandma perhaps?"

Good Draso, he had to bring that up. "Why would it be Grandma?"

"It's coming up on a year."

Ryuichi shrugged. "Maybe. I don't know."

"You're sure they never found anything?"

Ryuichi's ear twitched. "No. Nothing."

Trecheon fiddled with his hands. "You think there's a chance she could be alive?"

Ryuichi pressed his eyes shut. This was it. This was the moment where he could explain everything. Show them

Solas, have her play the recording, visit the plane, explain their whole past, play with some magic, try to get them to understand...

But imagining Trecheon's reaction to everything – the magic, the technology, the A.I., his grandmother, the madman threatening them, their own family's past as genocidal killers... he couldn't do it. He couldn't wreck them like that, all on the off chance that he might find his wife, alive, on a different planet, maybe.

Hell. How could he entertain the idea of dropping everything and wasting his life searching an *entire planet* for his wife when he had an obligation to protect his family here? Much as he missed and loved his wife, he also loved his grandkids. And they needed him.

She would want him to stay here.

"It's best to let go of the dead, Trecheon."

Trecheon breathed deeply. "You're right." He stood. "I'm gonna go back inside. Don't wallow out here too long, okay? Ayumi would never forgive you."

"Right. I'll be in soon."

Trecheon patted Ryuichi's shoulder then went inside.

Ryuichi shuddered, letting the tears fall as he stared at the stars. *I'm sorry, Solana. But I have to stay here. I have to protect our family. I can only hope you'd forgive me for that.*

Best to let go of the dead.

After the kids went to bed, Ryuichi made himself another drink and headed to the office, already prepared for the fight with Solas. She wouldn't be happy that he decided to stay here, but what choice did he have? She'd just have to deal. He opened the door.

"Ryuichi, thank Draso you're here!" Solas blurted the moment he entered.

Ryuichi slammed the door. "Not so loud, the kids will

hear you!"

"I don't care!" Solas said, fidgeting with her hands, her whiskers and ears twitching. "This is *important*. I picked up another recording!"

Ryuichi's vision blurred and his body buzzed at the news. "Tell me you're kidding."

"I'm not!" Solas said, breathing little tongues of blue fire in her agitation. "It's--"

"No," Ryuichi said. "I don't want to hear it."

"What?" Solas said. Her hologram sputtered. "But--"

"*No*, Solas," Ryuichi said. "I don't care what you heard. I can't go flying off to some foreign planet to spend the rest of my life looking for my wife who could be *dead* now, for all I know, when my kids are right--"

"But just *listen!*" Solas manifested her pearl and played the recording.

"*I'm not seeing any of our livestock with the name Ryuichi,*" said a familiar, droning voice. The same person who spoke with his wife in the previous recording.

"*Then why would she use the name?*" a feminine voice answered, almost concerned.

"*You know how they are,*" a third, deeply masculine voice spoke. "*You can't breed the stupid out of them. Believe me, we've tried.*"

"*Really?*" the feminine voice said, angry. "*Uncalled for, Kato.*"

"*If I may, Ayo-Kato,*" the first voice said. "*I see no similar species among our livestock. I believe she may be an escapee.*"

Ryuichi's muscles locked.

"*But whose is she then?*" the feminine voice asked.

"*I will ask around, Ayo-Kamaria,*" the first voice said. "*But in the meantime, we must feed and house her. If she belongs to someone, it would not do to return her dead.*"

Ryuichi shuddered.

"*A waste of resources if she has no one to breed with,*" the deep masculine voice said. "*Give it a month, and let's hope the owner is offering a reward.*"

"*And if I am unable to find her owner in a month?*"

"*Then send her to slaughter,*" the masculine voice replied. "*She'll be more use to us there.*"

"*I shall see to it, Ayo-Kato.*"

The recording ended.

Ryuichi fell into his office chair, flattening his ears against his head. Slaughter. *Slaughter.*

How could they do that? She was a living, intelligent, sentient creature. And they would send her to *slaughter?*

No.

"We're leaving tonight," Ryuichi said. He ripped open a drawer in the desk, whipped open a hidden panel, pulled out a key, and kneeled next to the office safe. "But I have one more thing to do before we go."

Ryuichi sat in his office and stared at the unbound Gem in his hand. Such a dull thing. It lacked the beauty and luster of his bound Gem. More like a dreary glass paperweight you'd find in pitstop town giftshops than a tool of magic and power.

He had been so determined when he first started this. He knew he had to get to his wife now. To leave her to potential slaughter was unthinkable.

But that didn't make this any easier. He was still leaving his grandkids, alone, unprotected. He was leaving them to Theron, if sending them away wasn't enough to save them. He still didn't know if he'd be able to find Solana when he landed on this new planet. He didn't know if he'd even *get* there fast enough. If he even got there at all.

But if he didn't act now, he never would.

The grandkids were about as safe as he could make them, with the exception of him here keeping Theron guessing. But his wife was in the most danger she had ever been since facing off against their son's murderer.

He had to go.

But he could do one more thing to protect his kids.

"I could show you how to bind him," Solas said, hovering precariously by Ryuichi's left ear. Her whiskers and tail moved in gentle waves.

"I don't want to stick him with a bound Gem when I won't be here to explain it," Ryuichi said. "It's bad enough that I'm giving him the damn thing. But sticking him with something that'll force him to outlive everyone he knows and possibly granting him magic that he'll never understand would be practically killing him myself. No, I'll just have to hope it protects him like it helped protect Sol."

Solas curled around the Gem. "Want me to show you how to activate it then?"

Ryuichi lifted a brow and twitched his snout. "Activate it?"

"It's how Sol used them," Solas said. "A partially activated Gem only has a fraction of its normal power and pretty much exclusively uses healing magic, but it's better than nothing." She lowered her gaze, her emerald eyes catching light. "But if he does ever bind to it, it'll almost guarantee he has healing powers himself."

"I have a Gem from Sol and I don't have healing powers," Ryuichi said.

"You're Black Bound," Solas said. "There has never been a Black Bound healer."

Ryuichi frowned. "Why not?"

"Because Black Binds are created in moments of chaos," Solas said. "Healing is peace, not chaos." She eyed him. "Stop stalling."

"Okay, okay," Ryuichi said. "Let's do that then."

With Solas' guidance, Ryuichi activated the Gem, just slightly. It whined in his ear, and turned a faded shade of red, though it still lacked the luster of a bound Gem. He took a deep breath. Good enough.

"Let's go get him."

"You sure you want Trecheon?" Solas said. "Ryota is the

oldest."

"Ryota can only see the negative in everything and he's too self-centered for me to trust him as head of the family," Ryuichi said. "And Ayumi is far too young to put this on her. Trecheon has the strength and determination needed for this job. He'll protect his siblings no matter what."

"I'll concede that."

"Good. Let's get this finished so we can go." He headed out of the room.

Ryuichi stood in front of Trecheon's door, listening to him watch a video on his phone. The kid really should get to bed, but he had admitted to Ryuichi that it was hard to convince himself to after months of strict lights out and wakeup calls in boot. He claimed he never regretted his decision to join the military, but he enjoyed the freedom to sleep and wakeup whenever he wanted, and he was going to relish it while he could.

If only his freedom was the same as safety. This decision would be a lot easier. He sighed and knocked on the door.

Trecheon answered almost immediately, looking slightly confused, though he smiled when he saw Ryuichi. "What's up, Granddad?"

Ryuichi tried smiling back but couldn't manage it. He perked his ears instead, trying to stay cheery as much as he could with this situation. "Figured you'd be awake. Can I come in? I have something for you."

"Uh, sure," Trecheon said and stepped aside to let him in. "What's up?"

Ryuichi sat on the bed and motioned Trecheon to him. "I know you and Ryota are gonna be shipped out soon and I probably won't see you for quite some time."

"Yeah," Trecheon said, sitting next to him. "I'll miss seeing you, but it won't be forever."

Ryuichi chewed his lip but didn't respond. Draso, for all he knew, it would be forever. Damn this whole thing.

Trecheon flipped both ears back. Ryuichi shook his head and smiled again. *Keep it light.* He reached into his pocket and pulled out the Gem. "I want you to have this. To remember me."

Trecheon took the jewel, raising a skeptical eyebrow. "This looks like the one you carry around."

"It's similar, but not exact," Ryuichi said.

"What is it? Some kind of novelty paperweight?"

Good Draso, why the hell was he doing this? How could he possibly explain this to him? Damn it all! "It's far more important than a paperweight, Trecheon," Ryuichi said, hoping he got across how serious this was. "It's… special. It'll keep you safe."

Trecheon stared at him, incredulous. "Granddad, I'm far too old to believe in good luck charms."

"It *isn't* a good luck charm," Ryuichi said. "Look… you just have to trust me. This is important."

Trecheon frowned. "Granddad…"

"*I don't want to lose you, okay?*" Ryuichi blurted. Trecheon jumped. Ryuichi took a deep breath and locked eyes with Trecheon. "Please, for me. Keep the Gem. Don't ever let this go." He pushed the Gem into Trecheon's hands and held them tight. "You'll want it someday."

Trecheon stared at him, ears flat, frowning deeply. "Okay. Okay, I'll keep it."

"And you'll carry it with you."

"Yeah… sure."

Ryuichi let out a breath. "Thank you."

Trecheon bit his lip. "Right."

The silence grew uncomfortable before Ryuichi stood up. "I'll… let you get to sleep then." He headed for the door.

"You really are going to miss your full nest, aren't you?" Trecheon said.

Ryuichi looked at his grandson, trying to take in this last

memory. His characteristic Omnir red, mixed with the black streaks of his Sol heritage. The blue eyes he picked up from his mother. The intelligent, analytical side he got from his father. The determined, no-nonsense attitude from his grandmother.

Ryuichi's eyes watered. He didn't bother to hide it.

"You have no idea, Trecheon." He shut the door.

This wasn't a great decision. But it was the best one given the circumstances. He had done what he could.

He prayed Draso would keep his grandkids safe.

The dawn rose slowly over the X-Zero on Sol Island as Ryuichi finished the final preparations for flight with Solas. The dragon A.I. hovered over the bridge's instruments as Ryuichi's Gem pulsed power through it.

Ryuichi took a deep breath, tapping the arm of his captain's chair. "How's it look?"

"Excellent," Solas said. "Hull fully intact. Air scrubbers working at 100%. Food and water stations ready and working. Ship drones have cleaned the halls and gotten rid of all the bugs. Power looks good…" she paused, frowning. "It's fluctuating a little, but it's steady enough to get us where we're going."

"How long 'til we get there?"

"I estimate three weeks max," Solas said. "The fluctuating power is going to slow us a little."

"Three weeks!" Ryuichi said. "I won't have any time to find her! Assuming she isn't dead by then!"

"I can try and push it a little and cut off a few days, but if I push it too far, we'll just explode in space," Solas said. "Or we'll destroy the engine and float through the void until you die. But once we get close, I should be able to hone in on her signal and we'll get to her general area pretty quick. In theory."

Ryuichi pressed his eyes shut. That was a pleasant picture. Why the hell was he doing this? "Push it as much as you can, but don't overdo it. What's this place called anyway?"

"It used to be called Syphon," Solas said. "Though they recently changed it to Sonus."

Ryuichi raised an eyebrow. "Why the change?"

"Better PR, considered what Syphon means," Solas said. "The ruling Androvox harvest energy from the other inhabitants to power their society."

Ryuichi flicked his ears back. "Inhabitants like Solana."

"It's mostly humans, actually," Solas said. "But yeah, Solana would face that too. That's part of the slaughter process."

"I'm really not going to like where I'm going."

"Unless you're one of the ruling Androvox, no one likes the place."

"Lovely." Ryuichi strapped himself in and glanced through viewing screen. Flecks of light caught the leaves of Sol's trees.

By now Trecheon would be awake, as his military training taught him to be. Soon he'd notice Ryuichi was gone. He'd wake up Ryota and Ayumi. They'd look for him, call the police, fail to find him, and probably spend the rest of their lives wondering where he was.

He couldn't believe he'd ever come home. Even if he did find Solana in time.

Almighty Draso, I beg you with everything I am… please protect my family. All of them. Solana… I'm coming for you. Stay strong.

"Okay, Solas," Ryuichi said. "Let's do this."

BLOOD MONEY

BRANDON FIFE

"We almost done Opa? I been sittin' here forever?"

"Of course not, boy, we've only just started. You know that." The old man smiled down at the diminutive child, perched in the ancient, leather-bound chair, worn smooth by the passage of time and countless occupants.

"Just lay back and relax. This will only take a few minutes."

"I hate this!" The boy harrumphed, a slight frown creasing his freckle smattered face as his tousled, dirty blonde hair shifted slightly with the movement.

"Hold still now, Jair. You don't want me to miss do you?"

"No, Opa."

"Tell me what you did today? Did you like the walk we took in the forest?"

"Yes! It was awesome!" His face brightened at the mention of the morning's activity, a broad grin replacing the frown and his luminous, green eyes opening a touch wider than before. "I had a butterfly land right on my hand. I could feel his furry little feet."

The old man stretched a thick, elastic band he had obtained from Old Hilda down at the market between his gnarled, chestnut hands and wrapped it quickly around the upper arm of the child before deftly tying a rough slip knot that would quickly disappear with a tug on one end of the springy cord.

"Really? That sounds wonderful. Squeeze your hand into a fist for me a few times. You just think about those little feet on your skin. What did they feel like?"

As the child clenched and unclenched his tiny hand several times the old man watched the spongy, indigo veins pop up in contrast to the pasty skin of his inner arm, a roadmap, tracing the highways that carried the warm, crimson life underneath. He gently touched the skin, rubbing across it with one crooked index finger as he determined the exact path the vein followed. He remembered when he used to do the same thing to his daughter, when she used to help provide for them, before-- -.

"They felt like somebody was tickling me with a feather, kind of..."

"Why don't you tell me more about it?"

"I don't know it was just...awesome!"

The child was so immersed in his memories that he barely felt the blown glass needle, sharper than any steel, as it pierced his arm, the keen-edged bevel slicing smoothly through the skin before infiltrating the pulsing vein below. Nor did he see the wine-colored liquid flowing into the shallow, rune encrusted bowl held by the old man's steady, trusted hand.

"There. All done," said the old man as he quickly retracted the needle and replaced it with a clean square of white cotton to staunch the flow of blood.

"Already? That was fast. I think you're getting better."

"Maybe. Now you hold this bandage until your arm stops bleeding and go in the other room to play. I bought you a new toy yesterday."

"Really?" He squealed as he pounced out of the chair and bounded away without another word his wiry body disappearing into the other room in moments, leaving a red stained bandage crumpled on the floor in his wake.

"What would it be like to be that age again?" He whispered to himself as he turned, the ache in his crooked back causing an inadvertent groan to escape his thin lips before dissipating in the stagnant air of the dilapidated cottage.

He looked down at the saucer of blood, now resting silently in his rough palm and smiled.

This will feed us for a month! May the Gods bless that boy! I best get this processed before it goes bad. Only have a few minutes now.

He ambled over to his walnut workbench, now stained and dented from decades of use. Tiny puffs of dust flew up from his shuffling bare feet, miniscule particles hanging suspended in the amber light of the dying day that filtered through the single, filthy window across the room. He took great care to not let a single drop of the precious liquid he carried fall to the floor as he set the bowl down gingerly on the bench, making sure to place the container well within the feeble light cast by the ancient oil lamp perched on a rickety shelf above.

He turned to a battered satchel resting on the outer edge of the bench and fumbled with the worn leather strap for a moment before reaching into the depths of the bag. When next he turned toward the now cooling blood, he held in his hand the object of their walk in the woods that morning, a tiny, pale flower, shot through with gossamer threads of lavender and indigo. An auryn blossom. Exceedingly rare nowadays, but the old man knew of a secluded place concealed out in the thorny woodland undergrowth where he could sporadically find the delicate flowers. This blossom was the key! Well, this combined with the blood of his grandson Jair, the only one to carry the magic now that his daughter was gone.

He set the fragile bloom carefully down into the blood, making sure that the remnant of the plant's stem jutting out below would be the first thing to immerse itself. The runes encircling the bowl lit up with a pale blue light, continuing to grow in intensity as the long seconds passed. The transformation never ceased to amaze him, and he watched with awe as the thirsty flower drank deeply from the liquid below, pulling the child's blood through its ruined stem and deep into the delicate petals, turning the entire blossom a deep scarlet that now glowed faintly with an unnatural, pallid light.

"Just one more ingredient now." The old man whispered to himself as he lifted a trembling hand above the glowing bowl and filtered a few specks of an unknown, powdery substance through his aged fingers and onto the auryn blossom, the final step in refining the blood that would be their livelihood for the next month.

The old man sat quietly, patiently waiting for the process to conclude as he pondered the life that lay behind him, the thousands of choices and decisions that had led him and the boy to their current circumstances. If only his daughter had lived longer, had been able to see the young man that her son was growing into. He reached one hand up to his eye to wipe away the single tear that seeped from the corner. Crying wouldn't help anything. She wasn't coming back. Not now.

A sudden deathly quiet awakened him from his reverie, cruel reality rushing back to weigh heavily on his aged shoulders, inescapable and inexorable as time itself. He reached out and picked up the silent bowl, examining its contents thoughtfully.

"Perfect! That'll bring a good price to the right person."

He shuffled back across the room to a dusty trunk that

he used to store some of their meager valuables, the bowl clutched in his hand, the flower within now transformed from its original white to brilliant turquoise. He placed it delicately into a rough-drying rack built just for the purpose and as his hand released its hold and the clay vessel settled into its resting place with a muffled *tink*, a heavy knock sounded at the door.

Who is that? I don't have any appointments today.

The thought flashed across his mind as he straightened himself as much as his arthritic joints allowed and moved slowly toward the single door that opened into the cobblestone street beyond.

"Should I get the door, Opa?"

"No, son, you stay in there and don't come out unless I tell you to. Understand?"

"Yes, sir."

It could be any one of his customers, and some ran in dark circles. He knew the regulars well by now, but there were a few new ones, unknowns that showed up at his door every week, more lately since the decay had taken hold more firmly.

The decay.

Ugly and unstoppable at this point it seemed, a dark wave creeping slowly across the land, leaving few unscathed.

He placed his hand into his pocket for a moment and caressed the dagger that lay there, dormant. The hard steel and heavy weight in his hand reassured him and he released it, content in the knowledge that it was nearby if needed.

He opened the door and a dark figure, clad in a worn, gray cloak and with a broad brimmed hat pulled down to shadow his face stepped through quickly and shut the door behind him with a nudge of his boot.

"Who are you?" The old man inquired, then gasped as the light from the single lamp on the workbench lit up the chiseled countenance before him and recognition blossomed in his eyes. He was growing accustomed to visits from increasingly more important people, but no one quite like this.

"I apologize, Duke Washburn, your highness. I didn't recognize you in this dim light. These old eyes aren't what they used to be."

The man looked about the cluttered room, his practiced gaze taking in every object it encountered and seeming to examine it all, accustomed to searching for anything that might be used to his advantage. He noticed an old scrip of paper, half buried under a pile of junk on the nearby table and picked it up.

"Dr. Antony Borges, Alchemist and purveyor of rare herbs." He read in his deep, practiced politician's voice. "I thought for a moment I was in the wrong place. I've been looking for you doctor."

"Well, you've found me. What do you need?"

"I...I need your help." The pleading in his voice seeping through in spite of a supreme effort to keep his desperation veiled.

"How so?"

"I can't...*feel* anymore. It's just gone. I try to feel things and I can't. It doesn't matter what I do. It seems that there's nothing left. I can't summon up anything. Love, passion, sadness, anger, fear...nothing. What makes me human seems to be slipping away."

The decay.

"I know some people, have some connections. They said you can help. That you have something."

"I *do* have something, and it *can* help, but I have a very limited supply and it's but a temporary fix."

"I don't care. I'll do anything." He reached into the deep pockets of his cloak and Antony shrunk back into himself in fear, grasping for the cold bulk of the dagger sequestered in his pocket, but instead of producing a weapon the Duke pulled out a fistful of gold and silver coins emblazoned with a semblance of the king's countenance. There must have been thousands of crowns worth grasped in the sweaty palm. "Name your price and I'll pay it."

"The price depends on what I give you. Give me a moment and I'll get my supplies."

"Yes, of course, don't take too long though, I have people waiting for me. I can't have anyone see me here. It would look bad, especially after what happened a few years ago."

"Don't worry, your highness. I'm the only one here and I don't say much. Besides, this won't take long."

The old man hobbled over to the trunk once more and bent down to retrieve what he needed. In a moment he turned around, a small rack decorated with multicolored blossoms grasped in his now trembling hands. A tiny, brilliant rainbow, glistening warmly in the wan light of the single lamp.

"Is that what I need? What is it? What are you going to do now?"

"Relax, your highness. All in good time. Now, why don't you take a seat in that old chair over there and expose your chest."

The Duke strode purposefully over to the ancient chair and sat down in one swift movement, doing his best to evoke confidence, but his wide eyes and quivering lower lip belied the fear roiling just under the surface of his calm demeanor.

"How much does it cost?"

"Two thousand. I'll give you a discount for this first time."

"That sounds reasonable."

"Let's start out with this one." The old man said as he examined an amber flower that he held cupped gently in his hand. "Are you ready?"

The Duke gulped, then pulled open his silk shirt exposing the pale flesh hidden underneath, his answer barely audible through gritted teeth as he responded.

"Does it hurt? Never mind...I don't care. I'm ready."

"It just stings for a moment sir. No reason to be so tense."

"I don't like magic. Never have."

"Look the other way then. This will just take a second."

He tensed up and a grimace plastered itself across his face as the amber flower was placed in the center of his chest and new roots seemed to shoot out from the flower's stem spreading out across his chest in a bright, sinuous web before dissipating into nothingness. In a moment he relaxed, the tension flowing from his body in palpable waves as he sank more deeply into the chair, and a throaty moan of pure pleasure escaped his lips, and an amber light, the same color as the blossom, shone forth from his eyes.

"Oh wow! Oh Gods!"

He continued to repeat the same phrases over and over for several long minutes as the flower's magic coursed through his veins and bathed his tortured brain. After some time, once the initial shock of the magic had dissipated, he was able to regain some semblance of control and he asked.

"What *is* that? What did you do to me?"

"I can't tell you too much. I wouldn't want to spill my secrets to just anyone mind you, but I can tell you a little."

He leaned forward now, interested as the old man lifted the rest of the blossoms for him to inspect more closely.

A myriad of bright colors shown like finely blown glass and as he looked more closely at the flowers spread out before him the Duke could have sworn that the colors contained within swirled and sparkled as if imbued with a life of their own. He reached a trembling hand out, stretching as if to grasp the power flickering before him, mesmerized by the exquisite colors, but just before the tips of his fingers made contact the old man pulled them away, alarmed at the sudden desire that flared in the Governor's eyes.

"Best put these away, too much light will destroy them, make them less potent."

"What are they? They look like auryn blossoms, but like none I've ever seen before."

"You haven't figured it out yet? They used to be auryn

blossom, but they are no longer. They are now imbued with pure emotions. They run through the blood of us all. You've heard the phrases 'Her blood boiled.' or 'His blood ran cold.' They are not just phrases, they are reality. Whoever coined them knew the truth that is within us all. Until recently that is, until the decay began. But I have found a way to distill them down into their most pure, raw form. Each color a different emotion, harvested at the optimal moment. The amber bloom I gave you is concentrated joy, and I was just able to distill some wonder earlier today. *That* one's getting harder and harder to find. The conditions have to be *just* right."

"How long will it last? What I'm feeling right now?"

"The initial rush, as I'm sure you have already noticed, has already passed, but you will feel lingering effects for several days, possibly up to a week before the magic has completely worked itself out of your system."

"I need more. Give me more!"

"In good time, your highness. I can't give you too much at once. If the emotion from my source is powerful enough when the blossom is created, it makes it even more potent... and dangerous. I've had two people die in that exact chair you're sitting in. There are some blossoms I've created that I don't dare use. The magic is too strong, it's too risky."

"It's just...I had nearly forgotten what it felt like. The damn decay!"

"Come back in a week and I'll see what I can do for you. Remember, I gave you this first dose at half price."

"I won't forget. I'll bring enough to pay."

"Good. Now you told me someone was waiting for you?"

"Yes...Yes, there is." He shook his head, the effects of the experience still evident as he wobbled to his feet, the now colorless blossom fluttering to the floor, dislodging itself from where it had rested on his chest. "I'll see you next week." He strode to the door, his cloak falling shut to cover the tiny spot of blood that was already drying on his bosom where the flower's roots had punctured him. As he turned the doorknob and stepped out Antony spoke.

"Your highness, there's one more thing. If you speak of this to *anyone*, your supply will be cut off...forever. Understood?"

He nodded once in agreement before shutting the door behind him and hurrying off down the dimly lit alley, dodging the detritus that littered the ground at his feet.

The old man walked over to the worn chair reposing silently in the corner and collapsed into its comfortable embrace, still warm from the Duke's body, and exhaustion suddenly crashed down upon him in an implacable wave. He hated it all. Hated having to deal with other people and more than anything he hated having to take his own grandson's blood just to survive. A grin creased his face and he silently cursed himself and what he had to do as the boy slipped from the lone bedroom and ran to his side.

"Opa, is he gone?"

"Yes son, you can come out now."

"Who was he? He seemed different."

"A very important man. Don't you worry about him though. Why don't you go and play with your new toy some more? I need to rest my eyes for a bit."

"Okay. I can do that."

"Good boy."

His eyes lit upon the case, brimming with beautiful colors and he staggered to his feet once more.

"Have to put them away. Light will destroy them."

He stooped and grasped the case to take them over to the trunk again, but he paused and instead turned once more to the workbench.

Might as well do a couple more before I fall asleep.

He retrieved a heavy sword hidden behind the bench and laid it down in front of him, refusing to look directly at the blade before him. He had never really liked weapons, but they had their uses.

He pulled out a well-worn, granite mortar and pestle and

his aged fingers retrieved a single blossom, jet black and permeated with an inky, malevolent presence.

Fear

He had made this flower the night that Jair awoke screaming as yet another nightmare tortured his tender soul. They were becoming all too common as of late. Antony wished once again that the boy hadn't seen his mother, a blade still protruding from her side, lying in a pool of her own blood as one of the first victims of the decay lapped it up from the filthy ground like a dog does water.

He shuddered as he banished the thought from his own mind, his daughter's broken body having occasioned more than one of his own nightmares.

He set his mind to his work once more, grinding the dark petals into a fine obsidian powder, stippled with flashes of silver and gold. He then used a tiny brush and, with extra care that none of the powder touched his skin, brushed it onto the edge of the sword before him. The sharpened steel absorbed the dark powder into its pores, glowing with a sickly light before hardening into a dark, silent line. A single, tiny scratch from the blade now would turn even the bravest of warriors into a blathering coward, incapable of any sort of defense as the fear took control of his soul.

Antony knew that he would never be able to sell fear, who would want it? But as a weapon? Antony's blades were quickly becoming the most sought-after weapons in the entire kingdom and he had even attracted customers from beyond its borders.

He retrieved another blossom, brilliant crimson shot through with streaks of fiery orange. He felt an unnatural heat emanating outwards as he placed it into the mortar and repeated the process.

Rage

The commanders in the king's army had taken to cutting their soldiers with rage blades before battle, usually the troublemakers, the berserkers, and the shock troops and pointing them towards the enemy. It had proven to be a remarkably effective tactic even though most of them ended up dead. A small price to pay for the destruction they caused. He finished the blade before him, letting the magic settle into the steel and harden before setting it aside with the other weapons behind the bench.

He reached down to the rack containing the remaining flowers and sighed when his eyes lit upon one bloom that seemed to sit all alone, separated from the others whether by some unconscious thought of his own or because of the latent power within it he didn't know. It was midnight blue, the color of a midsummer night's sky speckled with the silver light of a million stars. It was the first one he made from the boy's blood and as he absently stroked one of the delicate petals with the tip of an index finger, he was taken back to the night it was created, the night he had held Jair in his arms for hours. The night that his daughter died.

Sorrow

One of his most beautiful and horrible creations. Exquisite and coarse all at once. He banished the memory from his mind fiercely, burying it deep within himself as he gathered the flower rack in his arms, blinking away unbidden tears as he moved once more toward the battered storage trunk.

He was awakened by the harsh sound of splintering wood as a heavy body crashed into the weathered door, rattling the frame. His eyes blurred as he rubbed at them roughly, trying to wipe away the sleep while simultaneously grasping for the dagger concealed in his pocket.

A pair of green eyes, overflowing with fear stared up at him and he grasped Jair by the shoulder eliciting a sharp cry of pain as he bore down a little bit too hard for the small body to endure in silence.

"Listen to me, boy. Carefully. You go into that room and don't you dare make a sound. Those men out there are not friendly, and I don't know what they might do to you or to me. If you hear me yell, I want you to go out the window and run. Run as far and as fast as you can and don't stop. Got it?"

"Yes, sir."

"Go! Now!"

The tiny figure had just disappeared, and the door closed when another powerful blow tore the door from its hinges and three rather large men tumbled into the room. He snatched the dagger from his pocket slashing at his nearest attacker, the darkened edge of the fear blade grazing the man's cheek and leaving behind a tiny line that seeped crimson droplets that glistened in the dim light. His eyes widened and a horrid screech emanated from his throat as the magic took hold. He turned and knocked down one of the remaining men in his panic before clawing desperately at the wall leaving bright streaks of red as his fingernails tore loose from their roots in his madness. One of the men slammed a heavy club into the side of his head, leaving him a crumpled, but now silent heap on the floor. Antony tried to slash out at his attackers a second time, but his aged muscles responded too slowly, and the other two men smashed into him sending the dagger spinning from his hand and knocking him to the floor, stunned and unable to speak.

"Dammit! He got Bruce!"

"Doesn't matter. We have him now."

He struggled briefly but was pacified as he felt the ligaments in his shoulder stretch as one of the men placed pressure on it.

"Where is he? Where's the boy?"

"I don't know who you're talking about. I..."

His statement of denial was cut off by his own scream as something tore and snapped inside him.

"We don't have time for games old man. Tell us where he is."

"You can't have him."

"He's the key. You said so yourself when you were

talking to the boss. We know he's special and we need him now."

"But you'll kill him!"

"Got a big battle coming up. You expect us to be able to make enough blades with just a little bit of blood? We're going to need it all."

"   You don't even know how to do it! You'll kill him for nothing, just like my daughter died for nothing. No! I can't help you."

The intensity of the pain as the rest of what held his shoulder together tore apart drove him into the floor and he felt acrid bile rise into his throat. He tried to scream again, but all he could do was gurgle and cough. He tried to say something more, but a heavy pain, more deep and profound than that in his ruined shoulder blossomed in the center of his chest and swallowed him, crushing him into oblivion, and within moments the darkness had taken him.

"John, He's not moving. What's wrong with him?"

John knelt down and put his head to the old man's chest, looking and feeling for any movement and sighing heavily when he detected none.

"We pushed him too hard. Old bastard's heart gave out or something. He's gone."

"Hey look over there. There's another room. Maybe the kid's in there?"

They crept silently to the lone door nestled in the wall and on a silent count of three John kicked open the door and they both rushed in jostling each other out of the way. They looked around the empty room searching for their quarry, but the only things to be seen were a few beat up old toys scattered about on the dusty floor and an open window, the faded curtains fluttering silently in the night breeze.

Jair had been gone for hours, wandering the darks streets, and hiding whenever anyone strayed too close. He had run for what seemed like days after those men had burst into their cottage, sprinting until his tiny legs had cramped and his lungs had turned into liquid fire within him. But he really hadn't gone very far and later that night he had managed to make his way back to the only place he had ever called home. He stared at the empty doorway a gaping, black mouth, silently screaming its agony to the world.

He was petrified, terrified of what he might find inside, but he had nothing else, nowhere else to go. He took a deep breath, trying to slow the tiny heart that tried to beat its way out of his already tight chest. He took a step forward, then another and finally stepped across the threshold and into his home.

He scanned the room cautiously, the only light a dim glow emanating from the nearly dead coals languishing in the fireplace. Then he spotted the silent mound, sprawled unmoving in the center of the floor.

"Opa? Is that you?"

He rushed over to the figure and grasped the shoulder of the only man he had ever loved, rolling him onto his back.

"Opa, Wake up! I need you, Opa! Don't leave me alone!"

He shook the body vigorously, praying and sobbing, heavy, salty tears leaving tiny rivulets in the dirt of his begrimed cheeks before falling into the now sightless eyes of his grandfather. But he knew that the old man was gone, just like his mother. Everyone had left him.

"Opa, please wake up! Please...!"

He lifted his eyes and spotted the trunk across the room. It seemed to stare back at him, a threatening hulk squatting in the darkness and as Jair looked a wild rage overtook him, an inferno consuming his small body from within.

He scrambled over to the trunk and threw back the lid, nearly tearing it from its hinges as he snatched the flower rack from its resting place and hurled it across the room, scattering its multicolored contents.

"Stupid flowers! It's your fault! Your fault!" He screeched wildly as he dashed back and forth crushing the blossoms under his feet one at a time and leaving a rainbow of destruction in his wake until they were all ground to dust. He fell to his knees near his grandfather's body, weeping as he hugged the silent corpse and kissed the wrinkled, parchment skin of its forehead, now soaked with his own tears. He looked down at the shell that had once been his Opa, empty and cold, and his eyes lit upon a single blossom that he had somehow missed in his rampage, glimmering in the dying light of the fire.

"Told you he'd come back, John. Grab him!"

"Won't do any good. Look at him."

The two men stared thoughtfully at the tiny body splayed out on the floor next to the old man, a flower resting on its unmoving chest and its sightless eyes no longer green, but instead the color of a midsummer's night sky, speckled with the silver light of a million stars.

EKA THE DUSKWEAVER

M.D. WEATHER

CHAPTER ONE:
LFG

Finally. After two hours of waiting, a portal opened. Eka flung himself in and freefall into an engulfing wind until his momentum slowed and his feet touched down on solid ground. The world formed around him. White stone walls wrought iron fences, dead and withered shrubbery.

And fire. Lots of fire.

Straxton Heights, where the traitorous prince Arkenbraith drove a sword through his father's face, pinning him to his throne. Of course, the Royal Guard didn't accept him as their new king and cut him down instead. Now, he and his rebellious army wandered the burning streets as reanimated corpses—fodder for curious adventurers like Eka.

Eka pulled his hood down off his cornrows just in time for a burning ember to singe one of his pointed ears. He swiped it away and glanced around to take stock of his party:

A humanish warrior, a smolmanish assassin, an elvish priestess—she scoffed at Eka for being a dastardly Duskweaver—and a dwarvish ranger with an itchy wolf.

Eka rummaged through his bags and pulled out a lustrous obsidian orb and a silver crochet hook. He whispered a spell into his orb and swirled his hook in a figure-eight until it snagged on an invisible thread and pulled. A small hole frayed open in the space before him— a window into the Netherskein. In a burst of green light, a fire impala sprang forth.

White runes swirled across the orb, revealing a name Eka couldn't pronounce. Not for lack of trying, it's just that fire impalas communicated entirely in belches and sneezes.

The impala belched and juggled a fireball between four different sets of arms that jutted at odd angles from its back. The ranger's wolf trotted over and sniffed it curiously. It yelped and bounded away with singed fur.

Stupid rangers. Control your pets.

The dungeon was simple and took less than fifteen minutes to complete. In the end, the evil prince crumbled into a pile of charred bones and dust, and his king-father's ghost rewarded the group with loot from his treasure box. The party took what they wanted and charged through the end portal without so much as a thanks. Eka stayed behind to loot anything they'd left behind.

As he rummaged through a dead banshee's skirt pockets, a rift frayed open beside him. A veiny white tentacle slithered out and snatched the impala back into the Netherskein.

Until next time, Eka might have said, but that was unlikely. Demons weren't pets. They were minions, summoned at random out of a pool of millions. The odds of seeing the same one again were astronomically slim. Poof. Gone. One and done.

Until never?

Eka secured his pockets and hurled himself through the portal.

Chapter Two:
Zilve

A patchwork of pastel clouds loomed over the city of Brunosten by the time Eka returned. He headed for the junk vendor, stopping on his way for a cup of soup. The soup was disgusting, but it bolstered his health regeneration for an hour and made him feel like a king. After choking it down, he strutted next door to dump four bags full of innards and outerds onto the counter. He slid a glob of unidentifiable flesh across. The stench was unbearable, but the vendor, Groknikith, didn't seem to notice. She was an ogre, so maybe she didn't.

Plugging his nose, Eka said, "Out of curiosity, who would buy that?"

Groknikith tilted her head toward the soup vendor.

Eka nearly upchucked. He accepted a bulging sack of coin and went on his way.

Every day was a grind.

Join a group of adventurers. Enter a dungeon. Kill everything that moves. Loot anything bigger than a clump of lint. Then portal back to sell it all before doing it all over.

Eka didn't particularly *like* the grind, but he needed every coin he could get so he could buy the fastest flying carpet on the market.

And so, he signed up for a new adventure party. By the time a new portal opened, the effects of his vile soup meal had worn off.

No matter. This was an easy one.

Crystal Spires: a sparkling palace in the middle of a vast desert, populated by mindless cultists and an evil Duskweaver (let's be real—most Duskweavers *were* evil) who used to be a class trainer but now dedicated his life to trying to stitch a bridge between their world and the Netherskein, which would allow the Lordmaster to claim dominion over the Mortal Realm.

That would be bad, so Eka—a not-evil Duskweaver—created his own (much smaller) rift and chose a minion to summon.

He couldn't ignore the erotic masculine grunt as a Magic-eater leapt forth and landed in a crouch that afforded Eka a perfect view of its posterior. Eka's eyebrow quirked upward. The demon had purple skin, with darker purple stripes that ran south of its navel and disappeared behind a strip of leather that covered an obvious bulge. Eka tilted his head, reaching the conclusion that he really did not mind.

He looked up and met the demon's fiery amber gaze. Feeling his ears ignite, he looked away—thought he saw the demon smirk and looked back—confirmed it and redirected his gaze to his orb while his heart battered around like a bird in a cage.

The white runes spelled out the demon's name:
Zilve.

The warrior charged forth, bashing his sword against his shield, and slammed into a group of cultists. The cultists fell with ease, not standing a chance against Zilve's magic absorption or the assassin's interrupts. Pull after pull, Eka flicked his magic hook like he was ashing a cigarette, cursing everything with agonizing, putrid-smelling boils before crouching to loot anything that died near him.

"Every little bit helps," he said as he stuffed his pockets. Someone laughed behind him. Eka peered over his shoulder and met Zilve's burning stare.

Odd...

A sharp whistle rang out. Eka had fallen behind. He charged down the coiling ramp and rejoined the group at the bottom in time for the final pull.

They made short work of the Duskweaver, then expelled any demons that had escaped from the Netherskein and sealed it off. *For now.*

Nothing was permanent in these cursed dungeons.

As usual, everyone took what they wanted and warped away, leaving Eka to loot the paint off the walls. He crouched to root through some rubbish. Something grazed his arm.

He leapt to his feet and whirled around.

Zilve shuffled backward, raising his hands between them as if to apologize.

"Uhh..." Eka uttered. "Hi?"

Zilve's eyes moved across Eka's face, lingered on his full lips, then returned to meet his gaze. He spoke in what sounded like Demonic Danish. Eka couldn't understand, so he just nodded. Zilve smiled and hugged himself.

Eka blinked, hardly believing his eyes. Was his minion *flirting?*

A rift opened between them. A tentacle wrapped around Zilve's neck and snatched him back to the Netherskein.

Eka's shoulders sagged.

Something about Zilve had him intrigued. Duskweavers were not like rangers, who formed permanent bonds with their pets. Everything Eka had studied over the years, every spellbook and every tome, taught him that demons were vile, bloodthirsty creatures if they weren't under a Duskweaver's command, borrowed from the Netherskein to mindlessly perform specific tasks. They did as they were told. Nothing more, nothing less.

They did not bond with their masters.

And yet, this one had laughed and smiled and even attempted to speak.

What did it mean?

Eka approached the portal, surprising himself with how disappointed he felt to know that he'd never see Zilve again.

"Until next time," he whispered as he stepped through.

CHAPTER THREE:
UNTIL NEXT TIME

The next day, he did it all over again.

"I should have been a healer," he muttered as he fell into a portal, he'd waited nearly two hours for. As his feet touched down and the battering winds cleared, he found he was back inside Crystal Spires. A humanish priestess was dancing in front of a dwarven warrior, while a smolmanish sorceress wearing a pink cupcake for a hat loudly chewed a wad of bubblegum. The last member, an elven ranger, tumbled out of the portal, followed by his adorably rotund pet bear.

"Let's take the shortcut," the warrior rasped.

Without waiting for a debate, he hopped the railing and scaled down the coil level-by-level. The sorceress jumped after him. Halfway into a freefall, she blew a giant bubble and climbed inside, floating harmlessly down. Eka was next.

As a Duskweaver, he had a skill that allowed him to devour an elf's ear and gain the ability to fall any height without taking damage. Since he *was* an elf…

He peeled off one of his own ears and ate it, then jumped.

The priestess climbed halfway down before dropping the rest of the way, relying on the warrior to catch her—he did. The ranger smashed into the ground beside her, obliterating a floor tile.

Somehow, he survived. The priestess laughed into her hands before healing his catastrophic injuries. She turned to Eka and graced him with a warming heal. Over time, his ear sprouted back. Eka panned around, taking head count.

Warrior. Priest. Sorceress. Ranger. Self.

Wonderful. Everyone was accounted for. He raised his hook and orb and summoned. A manly grunt echoed out as a purple-skinned magic-eater leapt forth.

The ranger jabbed his fingers into his mouth and whistled.

Eka's blood ran cold.

His bear. Is still at the top.

Everyone whirled on the ranger as a rising cacophony of shouts and spell casts echoed down the spire. His adorably fat bear bounded gleefully down the ramp, trailing the entire dungeon behind it.

"Mother of purl," Eka whined, pinching the bridge of his nose.

Someone snorted a laugh. Eka looked back. His heart did a back handspring when Zilve greeted him with a graceful bow.

The warrior bashed his battle axe to his chest plate, snatching their attention back to the crisis at hand. "Be vigilant," he shouted, "the healer's gonna to have her work cut out for her."

Zilve etched a sigil into the floor with his twin rune axes and spoke some words in Demonic Danish.

The healer drew a sharp breath and stood up taller. "Whoo!" she squealed with delight. "I feel like I just had seven espresso shots. Let's do this!"

With a guttural roar, the warrior charged into the horde of cultists and insulted their mothers and their loser gods until they all focused on him. Eka, between shouting commands at Zilve, flicked his hook and cursed everyone with putrid boils and chlamydia.

Amid the chaos, he caught Zilve staring at him. He couldn't help but smile.

A plume of fire shrieked through the air and engulfed Eka. His flesh seared and popped, and he fell to his knees, stunned. The healer couldn't break her focus from the tank, barely able to keep him alive as it was. Eka could only close his eyes and accept his end.

Cooling bursts splashed across his face. He opened his eyes, found a blue light pouring over him and coating his wounds.

Life link.

Zilve's life energy was flowing into him. But Eka didn't have that spell yet, which meant Zilve had connected to him willingly. This was huge. Zilve wasn't just acting autonomously—he was choosing to give a part of himself to keep Eka safe.

A ping of warmth radiated through Eka's chest.

Another fiery plume rumbled toward him. Zilve charged through the flames and scissor-chopped the cultist's head clean off its shoulders.

"Holy mother of Goff," Eka choked out. He regained mobility and reapplied his curses. A cultist hurled a torrent of arcane blasts his way. Zilv dodged between them and crossed his rune axes, soaking the magic blasts. With them fully charged, he hurled them at the mob. The axes danced around on their own, chopping and chewing through a cluster of cultists while carefully avoiding friendlies. Zilve raised his hands and they returned to him with an intense *smack.*

Eka picked his jaw up off the floor. That was definitely not in his spellbook.

Recognizing Zilve as their biggest threat, the cultists charged him. Eka swished and flicked his hook, sending a volley of shadow bolts exploding across them, turning three of them into blackened slime. It was a spell he seldom used since it also gooified their loot, but he didn't do it for himself. He did it for *him.*

Zilve nodded his thanks. He was hunched over and breathing heavy. Blood ran like midnight dye down his arm.

Eka knew demon minions never truly died, but Zilve was clearly in pain, and Eka couldn't bear it. He could spare Zilve by recalling him. He gripped his orb, but hesitated. If he did this, he might lose him forever. There was no way he would be lucky enough to summon him a third time.

I could lose him either way…

He didn't have time to debate himself. A fireball ripped toward Zilve. Eka shouted the recall spell into his orb. A rift opened below Zilve's feet and swallowed him.

After the chaotic battle ended, all that remained was a pile of corpses, one with the warrior's axe buried in its back. The warrior sprawled onto his back and dragged in deep ragged breaths. The priestess and the sorceress slumped against the wall and groaned in unison.

The ranger chuckled. "That could have been worse."

The warrior kipped to his feet and punched him so hard he flew into the boss's summoning circle, triggering the pull.

Eka hurried to summon a new minion. He hoped beyond hope for Zilve to return. Instead, he heard a sultry feminine moan from the rift. A blue-skinned Magic-eater with thunderous thighs and a soft round belly leapt forth. Thin strands of fabric screamed as they fought to support the weight of her massive breasts. Eka's orb spelled out: *Bronnys.*

Bronnys looked between Eka and the Duskweaver boss but didn't attack.

Zilve's autonomous nature had him spoiled. Eka shouted, "Go. Fight!"

She groaned and charged into the fray with her axes.

The fight was a cakewalk compared to what they'd already handled. The boss fell with ease, and the rift was once again sealed.

A portal to Brunosten appeared at the center of the room. The warrior grabbed the ranger by his neck and flung him through, not giving him a chance at any loot. Eka slid his smelly feet into a brand-new pair of boots and chucked his old ones through the portal. Maybe they would hit the ranger on the other side.

Soon, Bronnys' rift opened. The tentacles reached for her. She slapped them aside and leapt through on her own.

CHAPTER FOUR:
RETURN TO ME

Eka had a quest to turn in at Moonshire—the only reason he would ever dare go there. Known worldwide as the Town of Debauchery, Moonshire drew visitors from all over to perform a variety of colorful acts on each other. Bards were very popular, especially ones with flutes.

Keeping his hands in the air, Eka pushed his way into the noisy, crowded inn. He budged past a sorceress elf and her water elemental, which had an octopus floating inside it. Eka pretended he didn't notice one of its tentacles was reaching up her—

"Asshole!" a smolmanish with candy-pink pigtails shouted over the noise. A table flipped, spilling a card game all over the floor. Her dwarven opponent gave a belly-laugh as he twirled his mustache and waved for her to pay up. She raised a one-finger salute.

Eka reached the kitchen with minimal bodily contact and headed downstairs. He stopped before a man with a dull yellow orb hovering over his head.

"Here you are," the quest-giver said, taking him at his word that he totally, definitely, positively slayed fifty ice trolls in under two minutes. Eka chose a pair of emerald gauntlets with gold accents. They fit snugly, the color popping against his sunset-brown skin, and made him feel more resilient. Satisfied, he bounded back up the stairs.

Despite Eka's hatred of raiding politics, he decided to try his hand. After thirty minutes of waiting, a silver portal opened. He stepped through and let the wind take him. His feet touched down in the safe zone of a floating necropolis. Seventeen other people mingled, while the raid leader explained which skills were allowed and which ones made him feel emasculated—he didn't say that, but it was the impression that lingered. He screamed that they still needed a healer.

Eka pulled out his orb and his hook. A fire impala would be the correct choice against reanimated corpses, but Eka's curiosity got the better of him. The raid leader paused mid-sentence to gape at his obviously bad decision as a Magic-eater leapt from the rift.

Pure joy flooded over Eka from head to toe as Zilve landed beside him. He flung his arms around Zilve's body and squeezed. Zilve was tall enough for Eka's face to burrow into his chest.

Ten minutes passed and still no healer. The rest of the party grew tired of waiting and bailed, leaving only Eka and Zilve.

Alone.

Eka stepped over to the railing and gazed down at the ruins of a city that had been overrun by murderous hornets. A clock tower jutted from the papery crust of a massive hive.

Coming up beside him, Zilve playfully tugged Eka's hood down, exposing his cornrows. His hand came to rest on Eka's.

Their fingers interlaced.

Zilve breathed a mournful sigh. They couldn't speak to each other. Demons of the Netherskein could only speak their own tongue. But right now, Eka's heart sang volumes louder than any love language. He gazed into Zilve's eyes, caught them flitting to his lips and back. Eka pushed against him and raised up on his toes. Zilve smiled and leaned in.

An immense bright green flash froze them in place and left streaks across Eka's vision. He squinted and found a single bulbous eyeball peered at him from the rift. *The Lordmaster.* A laugh rumbled forth. The Lordmaster lashed out and dragged Zilve back. Eka defiantly held on, pulling him back. His flesh sizzled as a tentacle wrapped around his arm until his hand went numb and his grip loosened. Eka cried out as Zilve disappeared through the rift.

He fell to his knees, holding his arm. He fished out a health potion and drank. But that could only heal his physical wounds.

Desperate and foolish, he summoned again and again, but they were different every time, randomly selected, the way they had always been. Eka couldn't say how Zilve had managed to steal the summon multiple times, but he had, and he'd done it at great risk to himself. That meant more than words or thoughts could express. And now Eka couldn't imagine it any other way. He didn't want to. He didn't want any other demon. He wanted Zilve.

The portal home flickered and buzzed.

Eka picked himself up. He had no choice but to return, alone and hopeless.

CHAPTER FIVE:
THE BRIDGE

Mindlessly, he went through the motions.

Curse. Shadow bolt. Shadow bolt. Shadow bolt. Curse.

He could no longer stomach the thought of summoning demons, enslaving them, forcing them into dangerous situations, so he didn't. Without his minions, his performance plummeted. Everyone looked at him like he was an idiot who didn't know what he was doing.

And maybe he didn't. Maybe he didn't want to be a Duskweaver anymore. Maybe he didn't want this kind of power. He now understood, unequivocally, that they were sentient beings with their own wants and needs and desires. Maybe it wasn't true for the impalas, or maybe it was. It was definitely true for Zilve, and if one Magic-eater could fall in love, who was to say others couldn't as well?

After that group disbanded, he mindlessly joined a new one. This time, he wasn't the only Duskweaver. They both pulled out their hooks and orbs. Maybe this time, Eka could convey his desire for his minion act freely.

Two rifts opened simultaneously. Two magic-eaters leapt forth.

One let out a familiar grunt.

Eka's heart swelled. "Zilve?" It was definitely him. But though Eka spoke his name, he didn't respond. Eka reached for his hand.

A fault line shifted in his heart when Zilve pulled away and followed the other Duskweaver into the tunnels.

The second demon idled at Eka's side, awaiting his command. He didn't act ahead of command, didn't do anything more than what was asked.

Neither did Zilve. He behaved as any other minion, even when his health reached critical. A trail of midnight blood lined the floor. His master never commanded him to defend himself, so he didn't. And he didn't flinch when an enemy assassin's blade pierced his heart.

A rift frayed open. As Zilve's body was dragged away, a laugh rumbled in Eka's mind.

Someone shouldered past. "Move it, nub."

Eka didn't want to continue. His heart ached. He returned to the beginning and stepped through the portal, leaving the party to their own.

He wandered the streets of Brunosten for hours, inspecting other Duskweavers and their minions, hoping to catch a glimpse of Zilve, though he was uncertain what he would do if he had. It didn't matter, because he never did.

Weeks passed. Eka thought of him every day, reminiscing on their brief time together. Sometimes he caught himself smiling fondly. He remembered how valiantly Zilve had fought at Crystal Spires, against that horde of cultists and that evil Duskweaver.

That Duskweaver. What a fool he was to try and weave a bridge between the Mortal Realm and the Netherskein. What was he thinking?

A bridge.

Eka drew a sharp breath.

After stocking up on health potions and cups of mystery soup, Eka convinced his class trainer to let him borrow a magic carpet.

It was a slow flier and took an hour of travel. He soared south, far away from civilization to a sprawling white-sand desert. Through the sandy haze, the jagged Crystal Spires appeared, glimmering among the Sea of Broken Glass. Seldom did anyone get to see the magnificent palace from this angle anymore, not since the archmages gifted society with the ability to simply portal inside. But portals required a full adventure party, and Eka needed to do this alone.

The magic carpet dropped him safely before a set of enormous double doors, then shredded itself into magic dust.

Eka went inside.

With no healer to rely on, he had to scale down thirty-two floors in the coil. He finally reached the bottom and folded over out of breath.

"Back again?"

Eka went rigid and turned toward the Duskweaver at the center of his ritual circle. His belled sleeves grazed the starry tile floor. "Foolish of you to come alone," he said, pulling out his magic hook.

Eka put his hands up. "I—I mean you no harm."

The Duskweaver's lip curled in a snarl. "Given our recent history, I find that hard to believe."

"You are trying to create a bridge to the Netherskein," said Eka. "You wish to bring the Lordmaster here. Why?"

The Duskweaver scoffed. "I care not for the Lordmaster. Everything I do is for…" He trailed off.

Eka perked up. "Are you trying to free a minion?"

A nod. "A foolish endeavor, but I wouldn't be the first to try. Many have entered the rift. Thus far, none have made it out." He narrowed his eyes. "Before the summon gets disrupted."

Eka stared down at his feet.

"I know why you are here," the Duskweaver continued. "I witnessed how your demon fought for you, how he guarded you with abilities unwritten in any spellbook. That only happens when there is a strong bond between weaver and minion." He smiled fondly, seeming to get lost in his thoughts. "Love makes fools of us all."

"Will you help me free him?"

"You know not what you are asking. One does not casually stroll into the Netherskein. There will be no loot. No sightseeing. No backup. And if the rift closes behind you…"

"I know it's dangerous, but I have to try. I will do anything."

The Duskweaver looked him over. "Fine. I will open the rift for you, but on one condition. You must find my love and bring her to me."

Eka nodded. "Absolutely, I will."

"I don't believe you." The Duskweaver flipped open a large tome and leafed through its pages. "I believe you will perish like all the others. But in case you don't, do know that if you return here without her, I will cast you back in and watch as the rift seals you in permanently." Eka gave an indignant scowl. The Duskweaver snapped, "I've died three-thousand and forty-two times trying to save my love. How many of those times were you responsible?"

Eka clamped his mouth shut.

"How deep does your love run?" said the Duskweaver. "How far will you go to save yours?"

Eka straightened his shoulders. The Duskweaver cracked a smile and said, "Perhaps you will be the one who changes the world." He found the page he needed. "My love—Her name is Bronnys."

"Bronnys," Eka repeated. "I remember that name."

"I know," the Duskweaver said dryly. "She delivered the killing blow to me while under your control."

Eka's mouth ran dry. "I'm so sorry…"

"Don't tell me you're sorry." *Show* me. Go. Bring me her shard."

The Duskweaver's voice boomed as he read from his tome. He slashed with his magic hook and tore open a fraying hole. Salty, humid air blasted them both, carrying a stench of hot, sweaty ass.

A loud bang echoed down the spire. An adventure party was coming.

Eka spun toward the Duskweaver. "Maybe we should wait until—"

The Duskweaver raised his foot and punted Eka through the portal.

CHAPTER SIX:
THE NETHERSKEIN

Eka's skin burned as he skidded down the tube like he was in a water slide made entirely out of carpet. He clenched his teeth. Fighting against momentum, grabbed a health potion from his belt—and lost it. It popped free from his fingers and disappeared somewhere in the tube.

A light appeared below him. He launched out at the bottom like a missile and slammed into a firm but flexible wall, bounced, and sprawled onto a shifting, unsteady floor. His missing health potion fired out after him and nailed him in his groin.

"Found it," Eka groaned. He popped it open with his teeth and chugged its contents. Instantly, his body and his balls felt better.

He rose to his feet and looked around.

At first glance, the tunnel appeared to be made of yarn. On closer look, the corded fibers writhed together like neatly stacked worms. Eka grimaced and backed away. His feet squelched on the gushy floor. He caught himself on the squishy wall, and it took every ounce of willpower not to hurl.

Grazing his hand along the wall for balance, he reached the end of the quivering tunnel and peered around the corner.

His stomach stretched away from him.

The cavern was immense, two halves separated by what might be a bottomless pit with a narrow bridge leading across. Eka kept his distance from the pit, grazing his hand along the disgusting, gooey wall.

He'd always heard there were "millions" of soul shards, but a million was such an unfathomable number. That was only truer now that he was seeing it for himself. *Millions* of purple soul shards were embedded into the walls from floor to ceiling. They were identical in size and shape—tapered at the top and flared at the base, each the size of his fist. Light swirled inside some of them, while others were dull and empty. Eka watched one fade from bright to dull. A demon must have been summoned.

Eka threw his hands up and let them fall to his sides. How in the name of Goff was he to find two very specific needles in this impossibly large haystack? And if he did find them, what if they were out? No wonder nobody ever made it out of here. Every detail was working against him.

Uncertain of what to do, he pulled out his orb and hook. He may not be able to summon directly into the Netherskein, but it was the only idea he had. When he raised his orb, he noticed something—the light inside the glowing shards seemed drawn to it. He moved it side to side, up and down. The lights followed.

White runes swirled across the black obsidian—several names at once, ones he couldn't read or pronounce. "Voidspawn," he whispered. He wondered if the demons were arranged by type. If so, that significantly reduced the amount of time he needed to search. Though, a quarter of a million was still...

Eka muttered a curse and continued down the squishy walkway, scanning the names in his orb. The naming schemes shifted to a different kind of unpronounceable— fire impalas. Eka grumbled. That meant the Magic-eaters and brimstone giants were across the bridge, on the other side of the bottomless pit.

He swallowed and started across. "At least it has handrails?"

His foot slipped and squelched on the sinewy floor. This time he couldn't contain the hot bile that rocketed up his throat. He threw himself against the railing and vomited over the edge.

A bellowing roar rose from the depths and resonated with the shards embedded into the walls.

Wanting to be as far from *whatever that was* as possible, Eka broke into a sprint. He reached the end and dove against the wall, pressing his back to it. He held his breath and didn't blink for two whole minutes as he watched the pit, until he realized nothing was happening.

He relaxed and dug his heart out of his throat. He returned to scanning the shards, glancing over his shoulder every few seconds, until his orb returned names commonly associated with Magic-eaters. There were so many.

"Come on," he pleaded, "Give me Zilve."

He flinched when the shards twinkled in succession. Ripples of light spread up the wall until they circled around one in particular. Eka barked a laugh and dashed over. He grabbed a knotty lump of tissue and started to climb up. He would grab Zilve's shard, and then he would find Bronnys the same way. But he had to go fast. There was no telling how close the adventure party was to fighting the Duskweaver.

Something wrapped around his ankle and yanked him from the wall.

CHAPTER SEVEN:
THE LORDMASTER

An enormous eyeball stared at him from the pit, framed by jagged yellow leaf-like appendages, like a sunflower if sunflowers were incredibly disgusting. Tentacles spilled from the edge of the pit and slithered over, wrapping around Eka's body and drawing him closer so the eyeball could inspect him.

"Mmmyesss," the Lordmaster rumbled in a dual-toned voice. "I know who you arrre and I know why you are herrre."

A green light flashed behind Eka.

The tentacles flung him backward. He skidded across the flesh carpet and tumbled to a rest at the feet of Zilve.

Zilve's eyes turned down at him, but they were void of his beautiful amber light. The butterflies in Eka's tummy bumped around in confusion.

"Demon," the Lordmaster rumbled, "killl the intruderrr."

Without hesitation, Zilve unsheathed a rune axe and swung it at Eka's face.

Eka rolled aside as the axe sliced into the floor. He scrambled to his feet and ran, pulling out his hook and orb. A rune axe flew past, barely missing him. Eka flung a shadow bolt at the giant looming eyeball. The Lordmaster absorbed the bolt into its pupil, completely unharmed.

The rune axe arced like a boomerang and flew back toward him. Eka threw himself against the wall to dodge.

The axe juked with him. It drove into his shoulder, forcing his breath away before he could cry out. As he dropped to his knees, his hook slipped from his numbing fingers. A tentacle lashed out and swiped it into the pit.

Zilve stood over Eka.

Eka looked into his eyes and begged, "Please don't do this."

Zilve whispered something. Maybe, *'I am Sorry.'*

"Kill him," the Lordmaster growled.

Zilve raised his axe.

Eka gripped his orb, felt the smooth obsidian in his palm. His hook was gone, but maybe he didn't need it. The hook opened rifts to the Netherskein. Why would he need a rift if he was already there?

Zilve's axe swung down.

Eka shouted a summoning spell.

A burst of green light sent Zilve flying backwards. A red-skinned Magic-eater tackled him against the wall, pressing her axe blade to his throat. Zilve shouted something, his voice straining. The red demon paused. She looked back at Eka and hissed.

Eka understood. He charged over to the wall and raced up the squishy footholds to Zilve's soul shard. He grabbed it and pulled.

His hand slipped off.

It was too slick. He would need both hands just to get a grip on it.

The Lordmaster let out a thunderous roar. Eka looked back. A tentacle wrenched the red demon back and sent her plummeting into the pit.

"I command you!" the Lordmaster bellowed.

Zilve charged and swung his axe. The blade grazed Eka's ankle. Biting off a scream, Eka forced himself higher. He kicked at Zilve's shard, hoping to knock it loose. Zilve swung again and obliterated another demon's soul stone. A plume of white smoke seeped out and clouded the air. Eka grabbed the hem of his shirt and wrapped it around Zilve's soul shard. Gripping with both hands and pressing his feet to the wall, he pulled as hard as he could until the shard popped free with a hollow *thoop*.

Eka fell.

The light returned to Zilve's eyes. He flung his axes aside and caught Eka, and they both collapsed to the floor. Zilve held him tightly and kissed his forehead and cried out in Demonic.

"It's not your fault," said Eka. He squeezed Zilve's arm. "I forgive you."

Zilve pressed his lips to Eka's.

The cavern vibrated. The crystalline soul shards rang and resonated. The Lordmaster snatched Zilve by his neck and wrenched him away, whipped him around like a dog with a helpless rabbit, and spiked him into the pit.

Eka's screams died in his throat. He clutched Zilve's empty soul shard to his chest. His soul didn't return. "No," he breathed. He grabbed his orb and spoke a summoning spell.

Nothing happened. He stared at the orb. Maybe it didn't work because his minion was still active somewhere? Without a minion and without his hook, what did he have left?

Bronnys.

He leapt up and shouted at the wall. "Bronnys! Where is she?"

Light rippled across the wall and gathered around one specific shard—

The one that had shattered.

Eka looked up at the drifting smoke, and the last of his hope withered away.

Zilve was gone. Bronnys was gone. What a fool he was to think that *he* would be the one to succeed where so many others had failed.

Love makes fools of us all.

The eyeball stared at him as he sank to the floor. Its tentacles slithered across the floor, reaching for him. "Now

I take what is mine," the Lordmaster said, punctuating with a low rumbling laugh.

Angry and hopeless, Eka took his orb and lobbed it at him. The obsidian sphere nailed the eyeball directly in its pupil and shattered into dust.

The Lordmaster emitted a deafening shriek and reared back. It thrashed around and crashed blindly through the bridge before dropping out of sight. A wet explosion echoed up the pit and throughout the cavern.

Eka blinked slowly, unsure of what just happened. He inched closer to the edge and peered over.

Down at the very bottom of the pit, something twinkled.

The twinkle of—loot?

"No way," Eka whispered in disbelief. "Did it—did it just *die*?"

Strings of white smoke—*Bronnys*—flowed past him and poured into the pit. Eka contemplated for a moment. He peeled off one of his ears and ate it, then jumped in.

Eka splashed into a knee-deep puddle of inky black goo. He slogged around aimlessly until his foot bashed into something hard. He reached down and pulled up a small treasure box.

Lifting the lid, he found a black-and-crimson Duskweaver's hook, and a matching orb.

A teeny tiny Lordmaster floated inside. It fixed its eye on Eka and folded its tentacles in front of itself like a petulant child.

The white smoke wafted over. It twisted and coalesced into the shape of a hand making a one-finger salute. The tiny Lordmaster rolled its eye.

"Huh. What are you doing here?"

Eka flinched at the voice and spun around.

CHAPTER EIGHT:
MASTER OF THE REALM

A humanish Lightweilder stood before him wearing enormous shoulder pauldrons and wielding a giant hammer. A golden aura shimmered around her as if she were standing in direct sunlight instead of the depths of nothingness.

"How did you get here?" she asked. "This dungeon isn't supposed to be accessible for another six months. And… Wait, is that the loot?" She leaned into ogle. "Fascinating!"

"Wh—who are you?" said Eka.

"I am Jordbara, Master of the Realm. If you've ever experienced short-term memory loss or missing time, it was me de-bugging you." She smiled through the slit in her helm. "Now, let's get you out of here."

"Wait—" Eka threw his hands up to stop her. "Not yet."

"I'm sorry, but you shouldn't be here. I must relocate you…" She flinched when the white smoke curled around her. "What is that? That's not part of the experience."

"That's a Magic-eater. Her soul shard was destroyed."

"Oh dear. That's not supposed to happen."

Jordbara flipped open a small notebook and scribbled into it. When he snapped it shut, the smoke condensed and disappeared into the blackened goo. Seconds later, Bronnys burst from the surface gasping for air.

Hope flared in Eka's chest. "Can you recover a demon named Zilve for me?"

Jordbara shook her head. "Unfortunately, due to the nature of summoning, we cannot assign specific minions. I'm sure you know this already."

"But... He's my... We're... I..."

Eka deflated.

"Ah. I see now." Jordbara sighed. "There is one way I could assign you a specific minion, but it will take some time."

"Please," Eka said, "I'll do anything."

"I see that. You're here, after all." She straightened up. "Anything else I can do for you?"

The goo rippled around Bronnys as she shifted on her feet.

"What of her?" said Eka. "I promised the boss of Crystal Spires I'd return her to him."

"Oh? That's interesting." Jordbara jotted something into her notebook and snapped it shut. A portal opened above Bronnys. She leapt through without thanks.

In a flash of green light, she appeared on the other side. The Duskweaver leaned into view with a great smile and tipped his head—right as an arrow embedded in his ass. He spun toward his attackers.

The portal fizzled out.

"We must go now," said Jordbara. "Please take my hand."

CHAPTER NINE:
SSRC

Six months later, when the realm's inhabitants woke from a deep slumber, Eka found himself in a new role. He rolled out of bed and shrugged into a newly pressed emerald robe with golden accents, slid his orb and his hook into their sheaths, and donned a pointy hat.

Two strong purple arms slithered around him from behind and gave him a tight squeeze. Zilve rested his chin on Eka's shoulder.

"You look incredible," he said in Elvish.

Eka tilted his head back and accepted a soft kiss. "*Takshal du halg,*" he returned in Demonic Danish. *Thank you.*

He pulled away to open the door to his brand-new hut beside Groknikith's shop. A sign in front read, "*Soul Shard Reclamation Center—Free the Demons.*"

"Are you ready for this?" said Zilve.

A yellow light flickered on above Eka's head. He looked up and smiled. "So ready."

EHI! RAGAZZINO!

IGNACIO R. LIMÓN

OCTOBER 31, 1998

High up in the trees of Linnton Park was the most remorseful crow this side of the Willamette. Tomorrow would mark his 136th birthday, or maybe it was his 379th? Regardless, he had nothing to show for all of his years alive aside from his damned and eternal friendship. Everyone else he had known and loved when he was still a man had long since died almost 3,000 miles away in Brooklyn. Today on the other hand marked the day he had fucked his and his friend's lives beyond all recognition and straight into the obscurity of time.

Pucker Faced Mike switched gears after the snaps of several twigs further down the trail echoed up to him. Beneath him a string-bean of a boy walked into view. He stopped to open his backpack and fish out a white bag with the spotting of some grease on the bottom. The man was young and *distracted. 'Ho shit! Is that a doughnut? No, it's a sandwich...maybe not? God damn it hurry the hell up and open the bag numb-nuts.'* Mike could barely keep himself clamped to the branch in anticipation. If he took off too soon the kid would bolt with the food in hand, and he would have to poke around the trash with the raccoons, *again.*

When the boy continued to stand there with the bag in hand surveying his surroundings, the crow called out, "damn it! Open the fucking bag you stooge!"

At that the kid looked up wide eyed. "Are you going to rob me?"

"What?"

"Are you planning on fucking robbing me over some doughnuts?"

"There's more than one in there?"

Before the youth said anything else, he hastily searched the trees for the rest of the murder. When there were none to be had he said, "no. It's just one … and it's mostly eaten."

"You're a shit liar, kid. Put down the bag and walk away."

"You're not my supervisor!"

Mike cocked his head to one side to look at the other like he was stupid, but before he slung another insult or demand at him, he said, "you can understand me..."

"Well yeah, it's just a thing I do."

Without another word Mike flew down to a lower branch so he could sit at eye level with the stranger. "What's your name kid?"

"I don't think that's any of your damn business." Under his breath the stringy youth uttered, "nosey ass crow."

"Don't be a dick, you should mind your manners with your elders."

With that declaration the boy with big brown oolitic eyes that were almost hidden under a crown of curly brown hair, squinted like he was in deep thought. "How old are you?"

At this the crow mused. "Now who's being nosey?" He fluffed up his feathers as if he was puffing out his chest with some scrap of pride. "I'm a-hundred and six tomorrow."

"Happy un-birthday?"

It was another modernism that the aging bird couldn't wrap his mind around or accept. "That's not a thing."

"Sure it is. You should know—— Wait, why am I still talking to you?"

Mike hopped to another branch to try to regain this shiny and scarce commodity's attention once more. "Because I think we can help each other."

"I don't need your help. I'm fine on my own."

"You're a witch with an invaluable passive ability, and you're just out wandering alone." A passive ability like this meant no spell work was needed to communicate his plight, so there was no fear of time running out or something going wrong. This boy could act as his mouthpiece, even if he couldn't work the actual spell to undo the curse.

"I'm not a child!"

This time Mike's words were laden with a scoffing tone, "what are you like nine? Do you even have any hair on your nuts yet?"

"I'm an adult."

It took everything in Mike to bite back a cackle before he said, "fine. Show me a mortgage, or some documents pertaining to some crippling debt."

"Fuck you I'm eighteen."

"Phfft, eighteen. What have you even been through at eighteen? You might as well be nine."

"I don't have to stand here and take this bullshit from you!" His arm was flung out to angrily end the encounter. Unfortunately, the minute he stretched his hand out to furiously wave the bag of doughnuts, it was gone.

A barn owl swooped in with a screech and disappeared into the foliage of the tree Mike was perched in. Mike cursed under his breath before he hollered up, "Chirk! Get your ass back down here and give the kid his doughnuts back!" When the owl made no such move, he hollered up, "he was about to share!"

With an empty hand and an irate stance on the floor of the forest park Dave yelled at Mike. "The hell I was!"

A rustle of paper could be heard before the owl laughed. "Possession is 9/10ths of the law *Antonio*." More out of curiosity than civility Chirk asked, "do you even know this kid's name?"

"Don't be a dick, give the kid his food back." Mike whispered to the wiry young man, "What is your name?" To Mike's amusement the brunette practically hissed back "Dave." Mike hastily tacked on, "and his name is Dave!"

"You and Dave can go eat a bag of dicks Mike; these are mine now."

"Wait, I thought you said his name was Antonio. . ?" This new crumb of news was more than confusing for Dave. He understood the concept of nicknames, but those weren't usually other first names.

Mike didn't put any stock in the question now that his attention was focused squarely on Chirk. "Don't worry about it, kid." To add weight to his position on the situation Mike threatened, "bring down the fucking bag before I come up there."

"No."

"Chirk stop being a dipshit and come down, this kid won't help us if he thinks we're assholes."

Dave grumbled to himself, seeing how the dispute had shifted to the two birds. "It's a little late for that."

Chirk being suspicious as ever, but slow on the uptake asked, "what do you mean help?"

"Have you noticed he's talking to us?"

"Yeah, that's kinda weird. Oh … OH! OH SHIT!"

"Yeah, now bring down the bag."

Reluctantly Chirk tried to advocate one last time to have a crack at his ill-gotten booty. "But I haven't had a doughnut out of an actual bag in so long …"

Thoroughly fed up with the whole thing Dave yelled to get the crow's attention. "TONY!"

Both Chirk and Mike hollered back in unison, "WHAT?"

Everything seemed to go from one great annoyingly confusing mess to another for Dave. But in the off chance he had misunderstood he asked for clarification. "Wait … Are you both named Antonio?"

Still staring up to the space Chirk had vanished up to, Mike said dismissively, "don't be ridiculous, I'm Antonio, he's Anthony, there's a difference."

"… is there?"

Finally Chirk dropped the bag before he flew down to perch himself beside Mike. "No hard feelings David."

"It's Dave," he said shortly, "this day is so fucking weird." Just as Dave was about to pick his bag of carby crumbs, a large Havanah brown cat with jade eyes zipped past him to snatch up the bag. He disappeared into the thorny underbrush to create a barrier between himself and the man.

Chirk let out a riled hoot, "FOR FUCK'S SAKE!"

Mike yelled to the quick cat, "DAMN IT SAM! GIVE THE KID HIS FOOD BACK!"

"What for? We can all split it."

Exasperated and at the end of his patience Dave said, "oh my god, Tony you're fucking useless."

In unison all three snapped back, "vaffanculo!"

"Wait. Are all three of you named Tony?"

Sam cautiously poked his head out so that he was visible to Dave. "It's why we have nicknames." Having missed a good chunk of the conversation before the cat inquired, "how are you talking to us?" His eyes narrowed as his hackles raised before imposing a question onto his friends, "is he Fae?"

Annoyed part of the conversation was going to have to be repeated for the latecomer Mike sarcastically said, "does he look Fae to you?"

"Not really, but how is he talking to us?"

Seeing Mike was visibly irked, Chrik chimed in to *help*. "He's magical."

"That doesn't make any sense."

Like always Mike acted as if he had all the answers. "It's built into him."

And like always, Sam challenged Mike's matter of fact-ly delivered information. "You can't work a spell like that without *any* magic."

Chirk tried to be help and put an end to the conflict between his friends like he had been doing for well over a hundred years now. His body wobbled as his head remained still while he said, "It's all on his insides!"

Now that everything seemed to devolve into a state of awkwardness that one only experienced when parents or relatives fought Dave interjected. "I'm right here. Stop talking about me like I'm not."

Sam crawled out from his fortified space with the bag in tow. He dropped it at the youth's feet. "Look, I'm sorry kid. It's not every day we get our hands on a score like this."

"Like doughnuts?" Feeling more than a little guilty now Dave looked to each member of the trio, who all looked to be ashamed to some degree. He sighed as he thought of how to remedy this whole thing before settling on something. "How about we start over? My name is Dave Cohen."

A queer kind of ease rolled over them after that. Mike took it in stride and started doling out proper introductions. With his beak he pointed to the barn owl and said, "that's Anthony Esposito, but we call him Chirk." For his quiet feline friend, Mike didn't want to come off as rude by pointing with his middle toe. Truth be told he wasn't sure the gestures of man still applied to him as he was. So he balanced himself on the branch to make pointing with his next longest toe to the cat easier. "That creeping bastard is Antony Baroni, we call him Slick Sam, but back home everyone called him Sam Hill."

Sam rolled his eyes before interjecting. "He's not going to get the reference Mike, it's older than he is."

"You don't know that Sammy, he looks smart." Mike found himself puffing out again like he had something to boast about in spite of his situation. "Anyway, I'm Antonio Catalano, but you can call me Pucker Faced Mike, or Mike for short."

"Can I call you Mikey?"

"Not if you want to keep your eyes intact."

"Jesus, alright." Dave wasn't sure how true this was, but after the ordeal with the doughnuts he didn't want to test his luck. A few minutes stretched out before the group before Dave said earnestly, "I don't see how I can help you guys ..."

In a long stretch and a yawn Sam put in his two cents. "It's just a curse. We think."

"You think?"

Chirk hunkered like a weight was pushing towards the ground. Since Sam and Mike seemed to be sharing, he thought he would offer up something of value too. "The broad we ran into was definitely a creeper who ripped meat wagons often and liked clouting. You could tell she was working that way regularly."

It took Dave a solid minute to sort out Chirk was talking about a woman, but what it was she did was beyond him. "I'm sorry, she what?"

In a huff Chirk added, "the woman liked to steal bodies, keep up kid." It never occurred to him the dated lingo he was accustomed to using with Mike and Sam would no longer be in the general public's collective lexicon. Dave said nothing to correct or educate the owl, instead he let the others have the floor.

Almost morosely Mike said quietly, "yeah, it was a 118 years ago to the day. We probably shouldn't have been out dicking around when the veil was so thin."

Feeling as lost as ever Dave jumped in for the moment. "So a dead chick cursed you?"

And now Sam was confused. He also found himself wondering what they were teaching kids these days. "What? No, the dead don't cross over on Samhain. The veil between our world and the Fae is paper thin. That Halloween cross-over bullshit isn't how it goes for Samhain."

With momentary and undeserved cocksureness Dave blurted, "faeries aren't real."

As he cocked his head to one side, Mike took a long hard look at Dave. "You talk to animals, that shouldn't be real, or possible even with you just being a witch."

"I'm not a witch."

Feeling somewhat left out in the conversation Chirk blessed the interaction with more of his words of wisdom. "Yes, you are, I have that weird tingly feeling around you."

Not knowing what that meant for him, Dave still cosigned to Chirk's declaration. "Oh, okay? Cool?" When he processed it a little further, Dave found himself stewing in his own mild annoyance. 'And this asshole still tried to steal from me after he suspected I could do some magical shit?' For a flicker of a moment he wondered if that unstated observation said more about him or the owl.

Sam could see somewhere in Dave's face they might be losing him with this conversation. He did his damnedest to try to redirect it in order to distract Dave. "We should find you a coven, or a teacher at least."

"I can't do more than talk to animals."

154

Knowing full well this wasn't how any of the witchy stuff worked, Mike shot down any additional doubt Dave held, *tactfully*. "That's horseshit, you have something else you're good at. You need to figure out what that is with help." All three of them had come from long lines of esteemed witches in the old country, with a passive ability as rare as Dave's there was no way in hell, he didn't have a knack for anything else.

"Why can't one of you just teach me?"

Shaking his head Sam halted the notion. "We can't. Well, we could do some basics, but you need to have someone in a body that can still work magic."

"Can you just get your real bodies back from the...Fae woman who took them? You said the veil was paper thin today."

Scrunching himself into an odd ball of feathers, Chirk sadly said, "nope."

"Why not?"

This was not how Mike wanted this interaction with the kid to go. Dave didn't need to know this about them. In Mike's mind doubly so, if Dave ever suspected there were consequences for trying to meddle in *old* Fae magic. "It's a long story."

"I have time." Dave sat down to further emphasize his point. He opened the bag in the hopes he could have some of his snack now. When he peered inside, he immediately felt a pang of remorse as his bag was no more than a broken mess of doughnuts. "I have snacks too. They're kind of busted now…"

Seeing where Mike was coming from, Sam tried his hand at leading Dave away from the hard truth. "I don't know that we really have time for this."

Unfortunately Chirk perked up at this statement to razz his friend. "Ha! What do you have some biddy or a bee to get to Sam?"

Had Chirk been within the right distance Sam would have taken a swipe at Chirk as he spat, "dannazione Anthony!" With Sam's scolding Chirk forgot his better nature and dove for the cat with his talons splayed. Both Sam and Chirk dove and swatted at each other as they slung more curses in Italian.

Dave not versed in a lick of Italian silently watched the scene around him fall into a bizarre kind of chaos. Mike seemed to pick up on this to a degree, since Dave's looked as if he was in the middle of a heated argument at a family dinner. In a vain attempt to salvage their moderate first impressions Mike snapped at his friends. "Voi ragazzi! Niente cazzate!" To his credit the pair stopped their scrap and settled around Dave, who stared back at him with wide eyes as he sat. The crow flew down from his branch to join them like nothing had happened. He cleared his throat and started in on his story. As Mike began the tale Dave found himself passing out the bits of the broken sugary snack.

As it turns out, the trio had come over from Italy as small children before landing in New York. Even as witches within the new world in 1862 their lives were far from remarkable. Mike, or as he was known then, Antonio's, fate had been slated for a loveless marriage to a stranger from Naples a few days after he turned 18. His birthday was tomorrow, and his friends thought one last wild night was in order. So they took a boat and several bottles of cheap wine out onto the East River. Though much of the shoreline was filled in over the previous years, there were still large pockets of wetlands and swamps.

As he rowed with Chirk, Sam made a confession. "I have a bad feeling about this … We should turn back Mike." The poor sooty light given off by the kerosene lantern gave his light cool brown hair and jade eyes an eerie look. Chirk on the other hand, just looked tired and pale, between his dark brown eyes and black hair, his skin looked worse in the colder months.

"You always have a bad feeling. We would never have any fun if we listened to all of your *bad feelings,*" Mike said as his dark brown eyes lazily scanned the shore. He brushed back a clump of black hair with a touch of irritation. The hair oil that had been gifted to him today was not doing it for him like the wax he typically used. His aunt insisted it was the newest and most popular product, so he gave it a try. Most of the women in his family fretted over this match, to the extent they were trying to present and truss him up like a fancy fowl for the dinner table. It didn't help his case that her family made it known they thought America was crawling with barbarians and heathens. To prevent any foolishness with his face he shaved off his mustache when his sister casually mentioned using a wood frame to preserve the shape of his mustache. He *needed* this night away if she was as uppity as the rest of her family. If she could prove to be decent and open to the changing ways of America, it might not be so bad that he couldn't slip out in the evening and screw around with other men anymore. But when his thoughts turned over to the matter of kids, he shuddered; they were noisy, selfish, and more often than not sticky with *something.*

Chirk stopped rowing, not content to cosign to either side entirely without something to help sway him to the more sensible choice. "Pass me a bottle." As Mike leaned in to hand him one, the glimmer of something caught his eye. "What is that?"

"What is what?" Sam sought out whatever had caught his friend's attention.

While they bobbed in the boat Chirk pointed to a lone flickering dot hidden in a wild tangle of trees. "That light across the water."

Whatever it was, wasn't of any interest or importance to Mike. "Bah, ignore it, it's a lantern or something."

Fixated on the same light Chirk had caught a glimpse of, Sam said, "somehow I doubt that. Look at how it moves."

Still showing no interest in the distant mystery sparkle, Mike dismissed it once more. "So someone is dancing or something."

In Sam's mind there was no way any such thing was happening in the middle of a marshy patch with it being as chilly as it was. "With a lantern, in the middle of nowhere?"

Being bored by the whole thing Chirk took up his oar again. "Let's have a quick look. Maybe someone is having a party?"

With a resigned sigh, Mike accepted the suggestion, while Sam went along with the endeavor. So Sam and Chirk rowed the boat out until they struck the shore of a dense soup of a swamp. At first glance the area looked to be nothing remarkable; and then they saw it, the faint orb of light bobbed over a small pond. They stood in wonder for a little while before Chirk boldly approached the edge of the pond. He took his cap off and leaned over with his arm outstretched like he had planned to scoop it from the air.

Being as apprehensive as ever about the whole thing, Sam desperately tried encouraging a different outcome. "Chirk stop!"

"Shh, I want a better look at this thing."

Mike stood there with the open bottle of wine in hand tittering in his inebriation. It made little difference if Chirk caught it or not. They would have something to gawk and marvel at if he did, but if Chirk fell in they would all have a good laugh before going home. As Chirk waved the ball of light closer to him, it dipped without warning into the water below.

"Damn it."

"Well that ends things, let's go home."

"Wait, what the —"

The pond became illuminated with the light of the strange wisp. Chirk was inclined to move away, until it gave way to the reflection of some lush woodlands, in the daylight. Without ever meaning to, Chirk lost his footing and stumbled forward. He immediately vanished thereafter, much to the horror of Mike and Sam. When he surfaced, Chirk was disoriented and gasping for air as he began clawing his way out of the chest high pond. He hacked up the water his lungs had taken in while he tried to call out to Sam and Mike. Where were they? More importantly what was this place? A splash from behind with a fit of coughs and swearing brought Chirk back to his senses. Mike and Sam had followed him in, so as they floundered Chirk latched onto them and started dragging them out. Once they were all on the shore they just lie there basking in their shock. They probably would have remained as they were for a little while longer had it not been for the imposingly statuesque woman who loomed over them.

Her garnet eyes set against petal-pink hair and warm chestnut skin told them she was most likely not human. Upon a harder study her pointed ears only seemed to reaffirm this initial thought. The emerald-colored silk dress she wore was odd to them, it seemed to be a tunic that stretched to the ground to cover her feet, while sporting huge flowing sleeves. None could make out her shape beneath, because the neckline came over her clavicles and her waist was cinched with a mint-green silk sash. At first, they thought her to be some kind of a nun with the pale green veil she wore, but the gold circlet beneath it seemed to suggest otherwise.

She smiled graciously before lifting each of them effortlessly to their feet like they were as light as very small children. A feeling of unease settled on the trio as scurried back from her. When they were a few feet from her, they realized just how large she was. None stood up to her. If anything all three found themselves craning their necks to stare up at her. Sam was the tallest of the three at 5'8", but she stood over him with three inches between her chin and the top of his head. For a moment she tried to beckon them closer to her with warm words none of them could understand and a gentle hand. But when each man began to eye the pond that they had spilled out of, she grew visibly cross. By the time the sense to run from her seized them, it was too late. Whoever this herculean woman was had been quick to draw out a very small glass bottle with an even smaller cork.

Mike, Chirk, and Sam had all but reached the water's edge when the pop of a cork could be heard. Wind rushed over and howled around them before they could comprehend the gravity of a situation. Once their senses returned to them, all three men started screaming after coming to the realization they had somehow been diminished. Though none could see her chasm of a smile now, each knew it was there with the way her eye twinkled and the corners wrinkled up with crow's feet. Even with the language barrier, everyone recognized it as a genuine expression of delight. Their world grew dark as the bottle was tucked up and away into the folds of her sleeve. And no matter how loud each of them screamed, no one seemed to hear them, or if they did, no one seemed to care. After what felt like a lifetime in the dark, they gave up on screaming in order to try and hatch a way away from this massive monster.

Chirk held out a hand as he demanded, "give me your shirts and coats."

Mike vehemently shook his head. "No way this is new."

Sam didn't need to be asked twice, he was already half naked by the time he asked Mike, "do you want to die?"

Mike let out an exasperated noise of discontent before he agreed with a snotty, "*fine.*"

All three of their shirts and coats were fashioned into a Bonafede rope with the help of Chirk's deft fingers and the bit of magic he forced into the fibers. This had been the common passive ability that had often fallen to the women in his family, not that he minded. It created an out for him for hard labor and allowed him to work with his sisters in their family's tailor shop.

Utterly bothered he was cold, and half naked Mike petulantly asked, "what are you going to do with that?"

With a shrug Chirk said, "tie her up?"

It was about now Mike realized whatever Chirk had planned was either going to make everything exponentially worse or fail completely. "How?"

"I hadn't thought that far …"

In a snap decision Sam volunteered for the worst part of the jailbreak. "I'll hold her. Mike, you can help Chirk bind her if she resists." This was the only way that made sense to Sam. His own passive ability enabled him to hold or move objects with his will alone.

So they waited a little longer, when they saw the light of day again it was within a strange kind of an indoor garden. All around them were grey hewn stone walls, but above them was surreal. It was a bright clear blue sky, and somehow behind it there appeared to be more stone. Lush green grass was dotted with wildflowers of all shapes and sizes, some even looked new to the men. To the far corner was a tree that nearly scraped the sky, beside it lay a still black pond. There were no doors or passages here. However there was a leaded window in the wall closest to them, to their detriment it looked to be locked and without a key. Most disconcerting of all, were the three empty glass coffins laid out on the ground.

Their captor uncorked the bottle to shake one of them out. To be sure he made it out first, Sam pulled and shoved his friends behind him with a single thought. His body toppled out onto the ground, no sooner had he touched the grass did he exhume his invisible control over her limbs. At first, she tried to break free of the unseeable binds, after it became clear she couldn't do that and that Sam was slowly trying to peel her fingers from the neck of the bottle, she called out a curse. Again Sam found himself shrunken beneath the gaze of the woman, but when he cried out this time, all that escaped him was the angry yowl of a cat. Beside him lay his lifeless body. Before long she shook out Mike, who became a crow; and Chirk who took on the form of a barn owl.

In Erlivia (as they came to know it) the trio watched their would-be mistress, Halcón, ascend the throne, wed, and have three children. Three centuries passed them, and the men could only idly standby as their mistress dictated the bulk of their time down to the last minute of the day. A week before their 301st anniversary of arriving to this strange country their bodies were dragged out before the court. The queen and her people would have their champion, the red witch; whatever the hell that meant. In her hands were a small heap of polished black stones no larger than the eye of a person. They seemed benign enough to each of the men, until a superfluity of priests carried Mike's open coffin into a ring of blood within the center of the room. Five of them each dumped a handful of gold dust in with Mike, while the rest dropped in various herbs that the spell had called for. Right before the last priest peeled away from the body, he dropped in a branch from the oldest tree in the sacred grove.

From the edge of the ring Queen Halcón called out,

"In the cover of night,
remove our blight.
See this man and reveal his true self,
pull away his impurities with a delph.
Lighten the load of his bones,
so that he may bear a weight greater than a thousand
stones.
Give him the perfect form,
and when the day comes, he will weather the storm.
Good Graces we are not wanton in this plea,
help us drive our enemies into the sea."

Mike's lifeless body sat up on its own volition, his big brown eyes bulged as he hacked up a thick ooze the color of pitch. The substance filled the coffin and took on a life of its own once it reached the top of the glass. It climbed up over his head and over the sides of the glass. It slowly grew in size breaking the glass beneath it, the mass spread out to the inner edge of the circle to climb the invisible wall that encased the somewhat sentient slime. In the midst of all of this the snapping of bones and the tearing of flesh could be heard from the center of the circle. A ceiling seemed to cap the whole thing since the sludgy lump formed a dome for what felt like an eternity. When everyone in the room thought it seemed like it would stay like this forever, the living darkness collapsed in on itself to reveal a brown massive horse-like creature with a long horn protruding from its forehead.

This empty vessel stood on cloven hooves, and at the edge of his chin sported a long goat's beard. His shoulder was well over Queen Halcón's head, by the time the substance completely evaporated. The crest of his head appeared to stop shy just of ten feet, but the horn stretched out a little past three feet. As huge as it was Halcón strode up to the edge of the circle and beckoned the animal to lower its head. There were no problems in this act … But it wasn't until the queen bestowed five of the onyx spheres on the horned beast did a complication arise. Each ball burned into the flesh of the dire creature to sink into the skull. At first the beast did nothing but stand there while this happened, and all seemed well. Each onyx orb took the slick sheen of an eye before lids formed around each of them. A white blight began to spread around each added eye, and with the progression came a need for violence fueled by unadulterated rage. Mike's old body decisively skewered the queen through her shoulder, the horn went right on through her flesh like it was a sheet of paper.

She jerked back with a cry and stumbled back as a thick blue powder was flung forth. With determined shakes and cries the creature tried to shake it off before sleep overtook it. Mike could only look on in terror as his body was dragged away in chains, to where only the gods knew. In spite of her open and bleeding wound, Queen Halcón would desperately try two more times to create a champion for her realm.

In chirks coffin a single stone from the swale closest to the ocean and the castle was dropped in. To everyone's panic the results of the second attempt were not far off from the firsts. The only difference being that Chirk's body writhed and twisted into a hideously gleaming and gold Basilisk inside of the murky mess. The queen bestowed three of the orbs onto Chirk's new body, and the same blight that took Mike's body quickly began to overcome the serpentine nightmare immediately. It swallowed four priests whole and poisoned a score more before it too was put to rest and taken to the lower levels of the castle.

When it came Sam's body's turn, a flower from the grave of the founding Fae of Erlivia was placed with it. Halcón reached into the sleeve of her gown to pull out a small leather pouch tooled with flowers and leaves around a crest composed of an eight-pointed star. None of the men had seen the crest or the bag prior to today. A murmur of dismay from the remaining priests told them this was allegedly powdered blood of a Grace. She opened it and dropped the last onyx eye into the dried blood before cinching it shut again. After that the leather purse was tossed in with the body from the edge of the circle. Once again, the spell was repeated, and the living void colored of pitch was coughed out.

When it came to be Sam's turn to watch his frame be pulled and pushed into some new and terrible thing, he left before anyone could see his tears. He would not see the tall and lean, elfin version of Sam that looked as if he had been born of some dream. At last the queen thought the kingdom had their champion, the red witch, but she was mistaken. For this iteration of Sam, was plagued by the same blight that spoiled her other two tries. He refused to acknowledge any command from anyone, but the girl with gold in her soul and hidden spells in her short black hair. So with gritted teeth (and a great deal of disgust), Queen Halcón ordered him to be laid within a glass coffin and sealed off somewhere within the walls of the castle. But before he could be put to sleep, he said this, "I will wait for the red witch, like everyone else. She will come when she is born again of fire and death among people of little cornfields."

After Mike had stopped the story Sam stared at him with his mouth agape in bewilderment. Chirk was too busy trying to choke down the last of the doughnut crumbs while Dave tried to process the Fear and Loathing in Las Vegas version of some Tolkien-esque sounding tale.

"You guys never told me what happened to my body in there."

"You never asked," Mike said quietly, "and it never seemed like a good time to tell you."

Dave wondered if they were in that hellish A Song of Ice and Fire knockoff, how was it that they came to be back in this world? "So what happened?"

"What do you mean?" Mike sounded almost annoyed with the question. He thought everything was pretty clear up until his stopping point.

"How the hell did all of you get out of there and make it back here?"

Chirk shook the crumbs too small to be savored from himself before he said, "that's another long story... We need to start thinking about dinner, the raccoons are going to be out soon."

"Raccoons?"

As he stretched his wings, Chirk elaborated. "Yeah, you know those handsy little bastards in masks." When Chirk studied Dave's face he could see the stripling understood the implications of what he had said. In more of a hopefully suggestion than a question he asked, "unless you have a better solution?"

"I'm an adult with a credit card."

HOPE TAKES FLIGHT

SUSAN ESCHBACH

Tessiana d'Tieri peered out through a crack between boards in the abandoned grocery that had become her home. The shelves had long since been stripped of anything useful, so the roving gangs stopped raiding it months ago, affording some protection for herself and a ragtag group of seven women and children.

She cringed as a starving toddler wailed and slipped through the store to the back room where the mothers and their infants remained hidden. The teen-aged mothers had scavenged old blankets and some insulation to soundproof the room so the babies' cries wouldn't be noticed outside. Roving gangs hunted for young boys to recruit as soldiers and young women to be used for other purposes. Every girl in the group was testament to their brutality.

Karlin nursed her four-month-old daughter, and Selena

tended her six-month-old. As malnourished as the mothers were, they couldn't produce much milk. Both infants needed some solid food, but a little milk would hold them for now. Putting an arm around Karlin's shoulder, she hugged the girl, at fourteen barely more than a child herself.

"I don't have any milk."

They all survived on the edge of starvation, and dehydration made it difficult to produce milk. These girls, and the young orphan boy they'd taken in, were her family now. Passion swelled in her chest, a love fiercer than she'd ever felt for her own family members, even though their presence reminded her daily of the fate that had befallen her own two sisters.

Though it had never been her intention, she'd become the acknowledged leader of the group. Besides, as the only one of four women without a baby, she was more… expendable. It mostly fell on her to brave the outside and search for food and whatever she could find that might be useful.

Sanji slid into the back of what used to be the fresh produce department.

"Good job. I was watching for you and I still didn't see you coming. Did anyone follow you?"

The plucky eight-year-old had appointed himself their backup scavenger, in spite of Tess's repeated warning of the dangers if he was caught. The gangs' training methods were brutal, more for sport than for productive learning.

"No. I was pretty careful. I'm sneaky, you know."

He was. Stealth had become the key to survival on Ramada, ravaged by civil war for the past ten years. Everyone in Tess's band was an orphan, except for the three babies, but if they let their guard down…. Tess had been fortunate enough not to become pregnant when she was caught.

Her face burned as rage flared within her at the memory. She pushed it down. She'd become very practiced at that. There was no point in dwelling on it. It was a fact of life on their planet now.

"Did you find any food, Sanji?" Tess eyed the not-too-heavy bag slung across his back.

"Not much, but I found a dead dog."

Not a very big one from the looks of the pack, but enough to give everyone a little bit. They'd managed to find a pressure roasting unit and had rigged a solar power source so they could cook small amounts at a time without being detected.

"Take it to Marja. She'll get it cooked up. You get an extra quarter portion for bringing it in."

He grinned; brown eyes bigger than they should be in his gaunt face. His hair was mostly red, with just a hint of the blue and gold streaks that dominated Tess's hair.

"It's okay, the babies can have my extra."

A child, and already the heart of a man, willing to let his own belly rumble to help the younger ones. Not all men were bad. Tess laid a hand on her shoulder and closed her eyes, calling to mind the gentleness of her father's touch before the war had ripped their family apart. He'd come home on leave once a year after he'd been drafted into the army. He was a changed man then—nervous, cold to her mother, a broken man. Even as a child Tess could sense it. That was the last time she'd seen him. By now he was probably dead, though in the chaos of the complete collapse of the legitimate government, there were no records or dependable reporting.

There was no future here for anyone—not for Sanji, and not for the babies who would grow up in this hell. In that moment, she made a commitment. Somehow, she would get this group off the planet, though she had no idea how she was going to do that. Starships still came into the spaceport on the edge of the city from time to time, but they could be freighters controlled by the gangs.

Marja deftly skinned the dog and carved it into pieces that would fit into the roaster. Tess gagged in spite of her best efforts to control it. Skinning an animal was one aspect of this miserable life she would never get used to. Choking down the bile rising in her throat, she turned to her left to pick a pair of high-powered viewers off a shelf and looked around at her group.

"Guys, I'm going out—down by the spaceport, so I'll be a while. Don't worry about me. You all know what to do."

She turned toward the door, but the tingle in her spine told her all eyes were on her back. The rest of the sentence was understood—*if I don't come back.*

After peeking through a crack to be sure no one was in the alley, Tess slipped out of the store through the same loose panel that Sanji had come in, sliding it back into place behind her. They had cut through a section of wall so that when the panel was in place, it looked like the wall was still intact.

Flattening herself against the side of the building, she took a deep breath, then slid along to the back. The street behind was deserted. Midday sun beat down on the pavement, battering the city with stifling heat. The gangs were too lazy to be out this time of day. They would be drinking, drugging themselves, and snoozing until early evening. Still, there were always lookouts on duty, and they changed locations daily, so you never knew where one might be.

She slipped the viewers over her head and scanned the nearby rooftops, searching both for human shadows and glints of light that might disclose the metal of a weapon. She saw neither, and scooted across the street to the opposite alley. The viewer lens adapted automatically from distance to close-up, but she could adjust them manually if needed.

For over an hour she zigged and zagged around buildings and through alleys, watching for any sign of life on the way. She spotted three lookouts and managed to circumvent them, reaching the spaceport as the sun was moving behind the tallest peak of the mountains to the west. It cast narrow shadows on the sides of the buildings toward the spaceport, giving her shade for cover and forcing any lookouts to face the sun when they searched in her direction.

She found a small, abandoned store with an alcove at the entrance, casting a deep shadow between the protruding walls. Sweat drenched her shirt and tickled her lower back as it ran down to the waistband of her pants. The shade provided little relief from the unrelenting heat, and fear raised her own body temperature even further. There were no ships in port at the moment, and she didn't know if one would come in today.

If not today, then tomorrow, or the day after. Whatever it took, she would get her little band of refugees off this damned planet. She waited for at least a couple of hours. Soon she'd have to give up for the day. It was too dangerous to be out after dusk.

As the sun disappeared behind the lowest mountain pass, a dark shape appeared in the southern sky, gliding in over the ocean. She shifted position, trying to adjust the viewers to focus on the shape, but they were already at maximum. Without them she wouldn't have been able to see it at all. A good quarter of an hour passed, the object barely gaining in size. How could it be moving so slowly?

Her patience was wearing thin. Her stomach ached, and there probably wouldn't be any of the dog left when she got back. She rotated her head to ease the tension in her neck. How long would it take that damned thing to land? Surely it couldn't be more than half an hour if it was already in sight. But then, she'd never flown in any kind of aircraft. They always looked like they were moving slowly, but they had to be moving faster than a ground roller.

Time ticked by as the shape gradually grew larger. When it started a turn to set up for the landing, she realized it had looked small because she was seeing it head-on. From the side it was much larger than she'd thought, a long, sleek cylinder—nothing like the ships built on Ramada before the war. It appeared slow because she'd spotted it at tremendous distance.

The last colors of sunset had waned, and she would be walking the streets after dark if she didn't leave now, but she wasn't leaving without finding out more about that ship, especially if it was from off-world.

To her left, an eight-wheeled transport with the top cut off the cargo section rolled onto the tarmac. It bristled with armed men and towed another cargo wagon behind it. Too bad she couldn't warn that incoming ship, but surely, they would spot the threat from the air. The rifles the gangsters carried wouldn't shoot far enough to endanger the ship until it was almost on the ground.

The armed men made no threatening moves toward the craft. The driver halted near a landing spot, and the vessel hovered above them for a moment, then settled into place just paces away from the transport. One man jumped out of the passenger side of the cab and strode over to the ship as a delivery ramp slid out from its side. A man walked down the ramp to meet the gang leader—he was not Ramadi.

A full head taller than the gang member, with a body bulk that no muscleman from her planet could ever match, the alien stood at the bottom of the ramp with his arms folded across his massive chest. The gang leader laid his rifle across the front of the carrier and raised his hands in a sign of non-aggression. From the looks of things, these two were expecting each other.

It figured. With no operational production facilities, supplies on Ramada had grown steadily scarcer, yet the gangs seemed to want for nothing, given their ability to recruit new members with promises of food, clothing, and other scarcities. With young boys to work the mines, they still had supplies of valuable minerals available for trade.

Tess settled down on her bottom to relieve the stress in her legs. She wanted to watch what they traded, and she wanted to get to that ship before the ramp closed up, if she could find a way to get around that carrier full of gunmen.

The exchange took only minutes. The gang leader called some of the men out of the back of the carrier. They levitated five crates off the cargo ship, then fitted another levitator under the cargo wagon and steered the entire wagon aboard the ship. A handshake later, the transport carrier took off for the inner city. The ramp was still down.

Her heart rate shot up. Now or never. She bolted across the tarmac before the transport was out of sight, hoping the lookouts would be searching forward and not behind. Scrambling up the cargo ramp, she barreled straight into the startled captain.

"What in pit fire and damnation are you doing on my ship?"

She really hadn't thought this through. What if he just shot her? Thank creation he spoke Alliance, the trade language used by worlds belonging to the Alliance of Spacefaring Planets. Hers wasn't great since she hadn't gotten to finish school, but it would have to do. If only she could get a few words out before he killed her.

"Please, could I talk to you for just a minute?"

She was short, even for a Ramadi, and he towered above her, eyeing her with suspicion. He checked behind her to see who else might be lurking around with a gun. "What about?"

"I'd like to arrange passage on your ship. For me, and... some other passengers. Eight people."

His eyes kept darting behind her. "Where are they?"

"I'm alone right now. They're in a hiding place. It's not safe here, you know that. We need to get away. Please! Can you take us?"

He pulled her away from the top of the ramp and hit a button to the right, raising it back up into the ship. Then he looked her in the eye for the first time, no doubt trying to determine whether she was legitimate, or stalling for an attack from elsewhere.

"You're right about it not being safe. So what's a pretty thing like you doing out here all alone after dark?"

Pretty thing. Oh gods above, what had she done? "Trying to get passage on your ship."

He frowned. "What's your name?"

"Tess d'Tieri."

"I'm Benek Tradon. Eight people is a lot, and I don't have any extra living quarters."

"We won't be picky. We just need to get away."

He nodded. "What are you offering in the way of payment?"

Idiot! She hadn't even thought about that. They had nothing... not even enough to feed themselves. There was only one thing of value she had. She was a striking beauty—by any man's standards. And she'd made up her mind she'd do *anything* to get her group off the planet.

She spread her hands out in a sacrificial gesture. "You can have me."

He leaned back in a visible double-take and looked her up and down. Then he shook his head.

"I'll admit that's a tempting offer, but no. I'm not that kind of man. Seems to me you've got a few too many of that kind on this planet already."

She sighed from way down deep. Couldn't argue with that one. "Please. You obviously know what it's like here. I've got three other women besides myself, teenagers themselves, with babies, and one orphaned boy. The gangs will take him if they can find him. And the women—well, that's why they have babies, if you get my drift."

He sighed, rolled his eyes, and shook his head. "Pit fire and damnation. A rescue mission. That's all I need. And I don't suppose you'll be bringing any extra food on board to feed yourselves."

"No. We will bring what we have now, and believe me, we're used to living on meager rations. We'll work, all of us, any way we can to pay our way. But please, *please*, take us."

"You were willing to sacrifice yourself to save them."

"I *am* willing. I swear to you, I will do whatever you want. But I want *safe* passage for the other girls and the children."

"Get them here before dawn. That's risky, I know, but I don't want anyone to see you boarding. I'll guarantee safe passage for all of you—even you. You're one gutsy lady, and I have no doubt you're as good as your word. We'll figure out some method of payment, at least enough to cover the cost of food for the bunch of you. Fair and honest payment. I won't hurt any of you, and neither will my crew. I actually could use one more crew member. I guess you're it."

Tess stifled her tears but couldn't suppress them completely. When she tried to speak, her voice broke. "Thank you."

"Yeah, yeah. Go out through that hatch over there." Tradon pointed to a small oval a pace from the cargo ramp that was barely big enough for her to slip through. "And you'll have to jump to the ground. I don't want to risk the lookouts spotting a ramp being lowered. "Here, take this com piece. I'll be able to tell from my heat sensors when your group reaches the edge of the spaceport. Wait for my signal. Stay silent until you hear from me—they could be listening in on my frequency. Got it?"

"Got it. And again, thank you."

He dismissed it with a wave. "Be careful. I don't have to tell you you've got a dangerous night ahead of you."

"Yeah, but at least now there's hope."

Tradon punched a button and the small hatch irised open. Tess slid through on her belly, grabbed the bottom of the opening as she went, and somersaulted to the ground. She crouched for a moment in the shadows beneath the ship, until she heard a voice whisper "go."

The moon would not rise for an hour and a half. She could move faster now that she could stay in dark shadows, but she still had to watch for the sentries, and the gangs would be out in force at this time of night. What if she didn't make it back? They'd never know they had a chance of rescue. Even if she made it, their group wouldn't be able to get back to the spaceport before moonrise.

Tess yanked off her boots. She'd risk stepping on sharp debris so her bare feet would be silent on the pavement. She set her goggles on night vision, but the lookouts would have night vision goggles, too. She'd run past only two buildings when a piece of glass cut her foot. She stopped long enough to yank it out and ran on, ignoring the pain stabbing up her leg. Bloody footprints. No problem—they wouldn't be easily visible until morning.

She ran a dark, shadowed maze, spotting only three rooftop sentries en route to her group's hideout. Vehicles rumbled through the streets, and the air reverberated with shouts and random shootings by gang members, her heart skipping a beat with each pop. A couple of screams told her not all the shots were random. The muffled sounds hinted the main action remained blocks away. They made enough noise that it was easier to avoid them than the silent scouts. She scanned every rooftop, every shadow ahead of her, heart leaping each time something shifted.

In a little over half an hour she slipped in through the makeshift doorway and doubled over, gasping for breath.

"Tess! We thought sure you'd gotten caught. Are you okay?" Marja wrapped thin, cold arms around her.

"I'm fine. I've got us a way off this planet, away from this hell. Gather up what you've got. We leave in five minutes. Marja, is there any of that dog left?"

"One little piece we were saving for you."

"Bring it. Anybody got any hidden stores they were saving for an even worse day than today? We've got passage on an off-world cargo ship, but I couldn't pay the captain, so we'll have to fend for ourselves as best we can."

Selena, her six-month-old in her arms, frowned. "I've got a little bit saved away." She looked sheepishly at the group. "You know, in case there wasn't enough to feed Sasha sometime."

No one registered any negative reaction. Any of them would do the same to save the babies, if they had the chance.

"But how will we get more food if we're in space? It's bad enough here. What will we do out there?" Tears shimmered in Selena's eyes.

"I don't know."

In her eagerness to get them all off the planet, Tess hadn't thought through all the details. Maybe the captain would be willing to provide them with at least survival rations.

"But this is our only chance. If we don't do this now, you all will spend the rest of your lives in this hell, and your children after you. Make your choice now. I'm leaving in five minutes."

"What about me?" Sanji sniffled behind her.

She turned, grabbed the boy and hugged him to her. "I would never leave you. We couldn't have survived without you. Bring everything you've got. Have you got anything stored away from the hideout?"

"Not food. Got some knives I found that I could trade with. I didn't bring them here, you know, because of the babies."

So young and yet so wise. If she could get him away from here, he might make a good husband someday. While the others packed what few items they had into bags, Tess searched the store for any remaining items that might be traded aboard ship. There wasn't much to choose from, but she found some old cable, tubing, and a few other scraps that might be usable for temporary repairs on a ship. From the far back of the store she gathered up six cans of out-of-date food that had been her last-ditch fallback if her group faced its final hours of starvation.

Minutes later they were out of the building.

"Selena, Marja, Karlin, you do whatever's necessary to keep those babies silent. Stick a teat in their mouths and give them something to suck on if they wake up."

The young mothers' eyes were wide with fear, and they hugged their infants to their breasts. Fortunately, at the moment, all three slept. But if one woke, invariably the others would. Tess took the lead with her viewers set on night vision. Sharp-eyed Sanji ran guard at the rear.

In the distance, gunshots of rampaging gang members rang out, punctuated by occasional yells, but most of the action had moved to another section of the city. Neither she nor Sanji spotted any lookouts until they were almost to the spaceport. Still her heart pounded. They couldn't be that lucky. Then a shadow shifted above them. Sanji shot an expertly aimed arrow from his handmade bow and eliminated the sentry, nailing him in the throat. They snuck behind a second.

The hardest part would be sending the whole group sprinting across the open tarmac. A voice in her ear reminded her of the com unit Tradon had given her. "*All clear.*"

Tess pointed her group toward the open space. "Move it—we're headed for that ship."

"*Starboard,*" said the voice on the com. Good thing she knew what he meant. She steered the group toward the side of the craft facing away from the buildings.

She flanked the group on the side toward the buildings, and Sanji ran backwards, watching for movement behind them. As the group broke into a run, the jiggling startled one of the infants and he let out a wail.

"Man on the roof!" Sanji yelled. Tess turned to see him stopped on the tarmac, taking aim with his bow. No time for heroics now—the sentry already had a bead on the group. Tess grabbed him by the arm and yanked him behind her. A flash and a boom from the gun's muzzle made them both duck, and a bullet whined past her ear.

Gripping Sanji's arm, she ran a low, zig-zag pattern, trying to throw the gunman's aim off. Creation must be on their side. Bullets struck to the right and left as they ran, but all missed their mark. While the shooter focused on Tess and Sanji closest to him, Selena and Marji made it around the end of the ship and out of range.

Another shot rang out as Tess, Karlin, and Sanji rounded the back of the ship. Karlin stumbled, and Tess caught her.

"Keep going. We can't stop." Even if Karlin had been hit, she had to keep going.

Tradon stood waiting at the top of a foot ladder lowered

from the side. Marja had made it inside and Selena was halfway up. She helped Karlin and stood guard as Sanji scooted up after her, then bounded aboard behind them.

"Anybody hit?"

Karlin frantically searched her baby bundle. "No, we're okay."

"I'm fine," Sanji answered. The other two girls nodded.

Thank heaven. Tess dropped to her knees, gasping for breath.

"Gear up," Tradon shouted into his com as the ladder lifted into the closed position.

Engines hummed and the ship shuddered slightly. Liftoff caused a mild sinking sensation and the landing struts retracted with a whine and a thunk.

Swiping away tears, she looked up at Tradon. "Thank you."

He nodded. "I gotta get to the control room. Cargo hold's through that hatch. Press the green button. That's where you'll all need to stay for the time being."

"Is your ship in any danger from the gunmen?"

"No. Not as far away as they are. But I don't intend to sit here and let them catch up." He strode off.

They gave Sanji the honor of pressing the green button. The hatch irised open into a large area ringed by skids of shipping crates, with adequate space for Sanji and the girls to stretch out. Tradon had told her his ship didn't have any extra sleeping quarters, so this would likely be their home for a while.

A sudden jolt knocked all of them off their feet. Screaming, all three mothers managed to hang on to their babies as they fell, but their mothers' screams and the crash to the floor woke the infants. Their wails echoed off the cargo bay walls.

None of them had ever been on a starship before—they hadn't been prepared for the sudden grab of gravity when their ride rocketed out of the atmosphere. Karlin and Selena crawled to nearby crates and sat together, opening their blouses to nurse and quiet the babies. Marja rocked hers, singing softly.

Karlin's infant pulled away and cried. She dropped her head and kissed her baby. "I can't. I haven't got anything, I'm too dehydrated. She won't nurse."

"I'll see if I can't at least get us some water," Tess offered.

Sanji tugged on her sleeve. "I'll go."

"No. I want you to stay here. I don't want to risk annoying the captain. He already knows me." Tess stepped back through the cargo hatch and walked straight into Tradon and another man.

"This is Harry Simms, my engineer. He needs an extra pair of hands for some maintenance he's doing. You're it."

Tradon jerked his thumb toward Tess. "Harry, like I said, she doesn't have any experience, or any know-how for that matter. But she's agreed to work for passage for herself and the other women and children, so consider her a member of the crew. I have a feeling she'll be a fast learner."

Harry held out his hand and Tess reached out and shook it. "I'll work hard and try to learn fast. But, Captain Tradon, is there any way I could get some water for one of the mothers?"

"We can do better than that." Tradon motioned her into a side corridor that opened into a galley, evident from a couple of tables and chairs bolted to the floor, food prep space, a reconstitution unit, and storage lockers.

"There are food packets in here—they go in the reconstitution unit, there. It reads the packet label and starts and stops automatically. These tubes are water and juice packets. They're labeled in Alliance, so you should be able to tell what you're getting. You're all welcome to what you *need* but do ask them not to be greedy or we're likely to run short on rations before we have a chance to resupply."

Overwhelmed, Tess brushed away fresh tears. "Thanks. Um, are any of these packets milk?"

Tradon frowned. "Can't the mothers nurse?"

"Yes, once they've gotten hydrated and fed themselves. Right now, I'm afraid, we're all running on empty."

The captain scratched the back of his neck. "There may be a few milk packets in there, but I don't have any bottles or anything like that on board."

"We'll manage. And Captain Tradon, I really can't tell you what this means to all of us. I know my unskilled work won't be worth that much to you right now, but—"

Tradon waved his hand to interrupt her. "Yeah, I know. But I made my decision. Now, go show your girls where the food is, and then meet Harry in engineering, through that hatch." He pointed to another doorway on the far side of the galley.

"And here." He opened a storage unit next to the galley and pulled out a stack of bedding and a couple of pillows. "I don't have enough for everybody. You'll have to sleep in shifts. And in the room at the back of the cargo bay, there are storage baskets the babies can sleep in.

Compared to how they'd been living, this was almost paradise. "Captain, this is so much more than I expected."

"And, by the way, just call me Benek. We're a small crew. No need for military protocol."

Tess nodded and went back through the cargo bay hatch to show Sanji and Karlin to the galley.

"Get yourselves something to eat and drink, then you're in charge of helping Selena and Marji. Captain Tradon said we could all have what we needed but tell them all to go slow. No more than half a food packet for now, even if they're still hungry. Our stomachs can't handle too much food at one time because we've gone hungry for so long. Understand?"

Sanji flung his arms around her waist and hugged her so hard she gasped. Karlin leaned over him and hugged her shoulders with one arm. Even her baby gazed up at Tess with dark green eyes, the first few tufts of blue and gold hair sprouting from her head like stray weeds.

"Tess, we love you. You can't know how much this

means to all of us."

She did know. At Sanji's age, she'd watched helplessly from hiding while a gang raped and murdered her mother, then took turns with her two sisters.

"I love you guys, too." She wrapped her arms around the two of them. "I have to go help in engineering. Be back in a while."

She pulled away and headed through the hatch on the far side. For the first time since her sisters' deaths, her heart pounded with love instead of fear. She'd have risked anything for them—*had* risked her own life more times than she could count. But this, her greatest challenge, had won them more than mere survival.

Now they had hope for a better future.

THE QUEST OF MEGAN WEAVERSDOTTER

CLEMENTINE FRASER

Snow lay heavily on the fields, as it had every day beyond count. There were stories that once the land beneath the mantle of white had rippled green and lush and the happy faces of flowers lay scattered like colored stones over the fields. Megan rubbed her face, icy cold and wet, the skin tough and strong. Stories like that were for infants.

This was further than she'd ever gone before. The valley in which her village nestled was far behind her, hidden now by the mountain pass. Hours had passed since anything other than the hardiest scrub had braved its face above the snow, but determination drove her onwards. No-one else would marry Donal Thaneson, not if she could help it. The memory of the sparkle of his eyes and warm breath on her cheek lit a fire no snow could quench.

Find the heatstone, bring it back, marry the Thaneson. Simple.

Her footing slipped, and she landed heavily on her knees. Pushing up against the staff, she brushed snow off her leggings and pulled her tunic back under her belt. Right. Simple.

She scowled and strode on, cursing the old Thane under her breath. Thane Merrick loved his son and delighted in setting quests. One week ago he gathered the people from the five villages and declared gleefully that none, but the worthiest woman would marry his son. Megan still wasn't convinced the heatstone existed outside legend. It would be just like the old man to send everyone on some doomed mission and then sigh as he declared Donal must delay marriage for another year.

Most of the other young women had gone off towards Mount Dunhelm, following rumors of hot springs and secret lairs. But grandmother had pulled her aside, tucked a worn mirror and comb in her pack, and whispered of voices that sang from the caves to the north.

Grandmother was right more than she was wrong, and the closest thing to a witch this side of the Brynderwyn Ranges. Trudging on through the endless snowy fields, boots beginning to take in the damp despite Ma's greasing, Megan wondered now if she'd made the right choice.

The caves opened in front of her, great chasms of black in an endless vista of white. She blinked and rubbed a trickle of sweat from her brow. Go in, find the heatstone, come out. Simple.

She stood, gazing at the deep black holes for longer than was comfortable. Donal's smile flashed in her mind, whispered promises in the forest putting steel in her spine. She could do this. Go in the caves, marry the Thaneson.

The air shimmered as she stepped into the gloom. She caught her breath at a sensation of a snare drawing tighter around her. *Nothing. Just my imagination.* Melting snow dripped from the cavern roof, and she scowled and pulled her hood over her curls. One strand was missing, lying tucked in Donal's pocket. The floor of the cave was slippery, but her feet were sure.

A golden glow pulsed up ahead, making her heart and her feet stop. Biting her lip, she waited for it to fade before inching forward. When it pulsed again, she grit her teeth and forced herself onward, slowly and attached to the cave wall, but moving.

Voices rang out, one booming loud and deep, the other a bright melody that caught at her heart.

"Sing for me, Blostma."

"I have not the heart to sing for you. I am chilled with sadness. Can you not let me go?"

The deep voice rose in an echoing bellow. "No! Without you, my heart will truly die." His voice softened and, despite herself, tears prickled in Megan's eyes at the pain in his voice. "Do you want to leave me so much?"

The bright voice sighed, and its sigh was a soaring tinkle of notes that spun around the ceiling of the cave only to drift sadly down. "Truly I would stay, but that my heart freezes. Soon I will have no heart with which to love you."

"I will make a larger fire. I will fetch the stone. I can warm you still."

Megan heard heavy footsteps and squeezed herself into a cranny, head down so her black hair would hide her pale face. Heavy red boots filled her vision, as they passed, they sparked flames on the cave floor, hissing into steam in the melted snow. Her heart thundered in her chest. There was only one being in their stories who took fire and ice wherever he went, the one who captured the sun's flame in the heatstone. Grandmother was right. The heatstone was here. As his footsteps faded, she raised her head and drew a deep breath, fear a cold trickle through her chest. Iren the Darksmith would not give up his treasure easily.

"He will not be gone long, lady. You should flee while you can."

Her head jerked up. Her legs wanted to run, but she could see Donal's face, disappointment twisting it, that awful Bryonny clinging to his arm. No, Megan was no lady yet but by god she would be.

She crept out from the cranny and towards the bright voice. The room was dim, the golden pulsing light had gone with Iren, but a glow deep in the corner drew her eyes.

It was a sylph. Tiny by human standards, with wings of a shimmering softness, the sylph wrinkled large eyes at her. The colors of the pixie-like creature made her mouth drop open and tears spring. She'd never seen such brightness. So many different hues that she brushed at her eyes, hoping to see more through blurring wetness.

The sylph rose, accompanied by a clanking sound at odds with the gentle frailty of her.

Megan gazed at where a chain, long and dark and heavy, encircled the small ankle. "He has chained you?"

A sad smile crossed the little face. "Yes, Iren believes he needs to keep me here to keep my heart."

Megan twisted her mouth and bit her lip but then blurted her burning angry thoughts out anyway. "If he chains you, he doesn't really love you."

The sylph gazed at her with deep dark eyes. "Do you not seek to join yourself with one whom you love?"

Megan flushed. "Marriage is not a chain. And if it is, well it is a chain that binds both, not only one."

Nodding, the sylph motioned at the chain. "This chain is made from his love. I cannot break it. For if I do, I will break his heart. But I cannot stay, for my own heart is dying."

Compassion flooded Megan. This beautiful creature could not be allowed to die. "I would help you, if I can."

The smile of the sylph scattered light and color throughout the dark room, and Megan thought suddenly that she knew why Iren could not let her go.

"He is bringing back the heatstone. If you use it to smash the chain, I will be free."

"And the heatstone? What happens to it?"

The sylph regarded her unblinkingly. "It will crack, the heat will return to whence it came, and the stone will die."

Megan stared at her. Get the heatstone, take it back, marry the Thaneson. Not so simple anymore. She couldn't leave the sylph here, not to die in this dark cave because of a god who would turn his love into a chain. Any marriage with Donal that rose from disregard to one in need would be doomed. And grandmother would give her such a scolding. But helping her would mean her own heart had no chance at happiness. Thane Merrick was always kind to her, but he was a man of his word—if she did not bring back the heatstone, she would not win the right to marry Donal.

Summoning courage, she set her shoulders back and met the sylph's gaze. "I will help. Tell me how to get the heatstone."

The sylph touched her arm quickly, a fluttery touch of shared emotion. "The mirror your grandmother gave you, do you still have it?"

She started and narrowed her eyes. "It so happens I do. How do you know about that?"

The sylph laughed, a bright tinkle that glittered in the air. "Here in the caves I have nothing but my voice. I sing to any who will listen, and your grandmother listens better than most. Does it surprise you that she hears that which others do not? That she sees where others are lost?"

Megan shook her head. Words wouldn't come. If Grandmother knew, then she would have known that the quest was doomed, that Donal was as good as lost. She had kissed her cheek and set her on a path to heartbreak. She glanced at the Sylph who regarded her, head cocked.

Perhaps Grandmother had her reasons. Perhaps those reasons were more important than one woman's love.

"Iren will bring the heatstone," the sylph said. "When he raises the stone, you must stand in front of me and snare the light in the mirror. It will blind him and then you can take the stone."

Megan licked dry lips. It seemed an uncertain plan on which to stake her life, but she dragged the small mirror from her pack and held tight to the wooden handle, carved with care by her grandmother's father.

The sylph darted a glance over her shoulder. "I hear him coming now. You must be quick and resolute."

Iren strode into the room. He filled the space with a looming bulk, his handsome face scarred by burns and weathered by snow. Dancing flames wove around his boots, and he smiled. An icy red light escaped his face, and Megan marveled that she could feel so hot and so cold at one and the same time.

The Darksmith raised the heatstone, and Megan leaped in front of the sylph, holding the mirror out like a shield. The beams of heat that escaped from the stone lanced into the mirror, bringing with them the weight of the earth. Her hands shook but she gripped it tight, dug her heels into the ground, and kept it aloft. The light wound around the mirror and flew back toward Iren in a rush. He cried out, dropping the stone, and holding his hands to his face.

She froze for an instant then scooped up the stone. A giant ruby glowed inside it, dark and hot. Crushing the rock would free the sylph but destroy her own heart's wish. Through a roiling tide of emotions, she brought the heatstone smashing down on the chains. Her hopes and dreams flew up in the shards, ripping her heart to pieces.

The sylph flung the remnants of the chains far from her. She fluttered up to Megan and smiled gently, the kindness a balm of sorts to her aching heart.

"Come, lady. We must leave now." The sylph paused at the door to say "Iren, my love, I must go but I will return when my heart is stronger, when the frost has gone, and warmth has returned. I promise you this." Megan turned her gaze from the heartbreak in the couple's eyes, pushing her own cracking heart away.

The glare of sunlight on snow hit Megan's eyes with a spearing pain. The sylph stopped, breathless and shaking, her gaze raking the vista of endless white. "No. Have I been his prisoner this long?"

Megan shrugged, the hollowness in her chest tearing at her thoughts. She was happy for the sylph's freedom, of course, but Donal filled her head. She sighed a breath that rose from her toes. At least that awful Bryonny wouldn't have the stone either.

The sylph took her hand. "I did not know how bad things had become. I must ask one more favor of you lady, if you would give it."

She forced a smile. "Of course, ask."

"My wings are tired from disuse. Would you hold me up as I sing?"

Megan lifted the sylph up high like a baby, tiny and light as she was. The song she sang seemed to reach into the bones of the earth. Energy pulsed through Megan's arms and feet, winding around her until she could smell it, hot and earthy. It filled the emptiness in her heart and slowed her racing thoughts.

The snow began to disappear. It didn't melt, it just no longer *was*. The song grew louder, stronger. Green grass thrust its way up through the parched earth. As the fields grew, waving fronds reaching to the sky, the sylph's wings grew stronger, and with a smile, she launched herself from Megan's arms. Everywhere she flew, small bright flowers dropped and settled in the field, scattering like jewels in the carpet of green.

Megan's tears flowed freely. There had never been such color in all her world.

The sylph landed at her feet, and she crouched down to look her in the eyes.

"How? How did you do this?

"I am Blostma, guardian of the green fields. They lay hidden and sleeping while I was chained in Iren's home, but now I have woken them."

A spark of hope lit in Megan's blood. "And we will have green fields forever?"

The sylph shook her head sadly. "No. For I too must honor my heart, and it lies still in Iren's caves. I will visit him, and when I do, the snow will fall. But I will always return. You will know I have by the flowers that spring from the earth."

Megan reached out and touched a petal of a bright red bud. Her hand trembled, and she drew it back.

The sylph smiled. "But I must go now, you have one who would speak with you."

Megan looked up, but the sylph had faded, her melody turning into the frantic calls of someone whose heart Megan still kept, though her own was battered and lacking in hope.

She rose and met Donal as he came to a stumbling halt beside her.

"Meg, you're safe! I heard you'd gone to the caves. There is a great godly beast in there you must never disturb." His gaze was on her face, such warmth in his eyes that she felt the cracks in her heart begin to patch up. Still, there was something she had to tell him.

"Donal, I lost the heatstone. I had it in my grasp, and I gave it up."

He looked, as if for the first time, at the lush fields around them. "Was it you who made this happen?"

"No, it was a sylph. But to save her, I gave up the heatstone." Her lip trembled. "I lost you."

He smiled, melting the ice inside her. "Oh, Megan Weaversdotter, you haven't lost me. My father can go on all he likes about quests and proving one's worth, but you've proven your worth to me a hundred times before today. I can only hope that I am as worthy in your eyes."

190

His arms wrapped around her, and Megan's heart sang as he kissed her. She felt her song echo in the soft wings of the sylph, and when she looked away from her love, it was to see silver wings fade and a smile, like a promise, curl through the sky.

TALON'S LOVE

ANDREW M. FERRELL

The bell jingled as Aleck pushed the wooden door open. He winced at the sound. An older man looked up from a box on the far counter. "Herb, poultice, or potion?"

"I'm afraid I need something a little stronger than that," Aleck replied. He slid his hood back to reveal shoulder length raven colored hair. He turned sea grey eyes towards the man. "I know you have more than plants and animal parts in this shop. I know you have ties to the Academy in Nishwam."

"I've put all that behind me," the old man said dismissively. "Even for you. Lord Aleck, Talon Knight of Bealck, Swordarm of Queen Isa..."

"Stop," Aleck interrupted. "There won't be a Queen if we don't get these two puffed up Chieftains off our doorstep. They're planning to turn her into little more than a member of their harem." Aleck closed the distance as he spoke. "I won't let that happen." He slammed his fist on the

193

counter. "Now. Help me defeat them."

"Even at my best, in my younger years," the old man started, before a coughing fit doubled him over. He waved off the concerned hand Aleck extended. The old man grabbed a nearby flask and sipped. "What you need is godlike powers. Or at least a demigod."

"I'm as devoted to Sotestari as any other warrior. But there is no way the God of War is going to help," Aleck said.

"But the Heabel may be able to help you," the old man replied. He sipped again before continuing, "He has magic nearly as strong as the Gods. If he'll meet with you, and you can strike a deal with him, it may just save our Queen."

"The Heabel? An old wife's tale. The Dealmaker is not a solution, he's a fantasy," Aleck said. He started for the door.

"Take this candle," the old man said, tossing him a stick of blue wax. Aleck caught it deftly. "Light it tonight. In the smoke, if the Heabel agrees to meet with you, there will be a location to meet. If you see nothing, then may Sotestari guide all of our soldiers in the coming battle."

Aleck considered the candle as he returned to the castle. An afternoon of troop and supply reports waited for him in his study, but perhaps they wouldn't be necessary. If only he could obtain an audience with the demigod of contracts.

Lord Aleck adjusted his plain brown hooded cloak and entered the dockside tavern. His piercing sea grey eyes scanned the room, not meeting any of the glances a new arrival usually garnered. The siege entered its third month, and even these hardiest of souls began to despair.

Aleck heard talk from one drunkard, criticizing Queen Isadore for not picking a new King and ending the siege. "She needs a King. Bealck deserves a King and she should just get on with choosing a new bed partner."

Before Aleck's blood boiled over at the insult, a burly sailor stood up, "What did ya say about our Queen? I'll gut ya like the bloated fish ya are."

Aleck took a deep breath and circled around the pair as their exchange heated up. He reached the corner table and found a young man with sandy blonde hair eating voraciously.

"Sit down, friend," the man said, pausing to lick juices from his hand. "You don't want to attract attention, do you?"

He sat, keeping his hood drawn over his raven-colored hair. He'd been careful in his attire, even leaving the signet rings of his House and station behind. "Are you the one who can help me? Are you Heabel?"

"Close your mouth, fool," Heabel hissed. He scanned the room, looking for any patrons not focused on their own business. Luckily, the sailor and the drunkard still exchanged words. Fists would soon join the conversation, however. Heabel eyed Aleck. "Do not use my name out loud," he said. "I'm here to make one deal only tonight, not bargain with a tavern of drunks. He picked up his leg of mutton. "What brings you calling?"

"I need to defend my Queen from these barbarians," Aleck replied, his voice heated. He looked as the conversation escalated into fisticuffs. The sailor made short work of the drunkard and cheers broke out as the man was dragged out to the street, minus what was left of his coin purse. The fool's money would be spent filling the cups of everyone else for his insult to the Queen.

"You don't think a young and pretty Queen, such as she, needs a King?" Heabel asked, knowing already of Aleck's feelings for Isadore. He froze when a knife appeared at his throat. "Not a good way to start the bargaining."

"Don't try your mind games with me, trickster," Aleck warned, pressing the blade against Heabel's neck. "I know how this works and I'm running out of time. Both of these puffed up tribal warchiefs want an answer by morning or they attack the city. I need a way to stop them and expel them from our borders. Now, name your terms."

Heabel straightened, heedless of the blade at his throat. "Calm down. I can help you. Do you love your Queen?" He knew the answer, but a verbal confirmation assisted in the magic he was already considering.

"With every bit of my soul," Aleck replied fervently.

The intensity in the general's eyes gave Heabel pause. "Does your Queen feel the same?" he asked slowly, studying the man across from him.

Aleck hesitated. "*She loves me, we just can't declare it openly. She's a Queen and I'm a soldier, can we be together?*" He swallowed hard before speaking aloud, "Without question." Aleck's words lacked some of the same conviction as his own declaration. "I have no doubts of her love or commitment," he added, pushing more belief into his voice.

"Hold onto that," Heabel said. "When you return to your chambers, you will find your armor and weapons imbued with the strength of your conviction. You will be invulnerable as long as you hold onto it. Speak not a word of this to anyone or the magic fails. Lose faith, and it fails. Understood?"

"I understand," Aleck replied, the wheels of a plan already rolling in his mind. "And what do I owe for this? You never give anything away for free. I'm no fool."

"I have a soft spot for true love," Heabel replied gently. He smiled and reached out his hand to Aleck. They shook, the grin never leaving Heabel's face. "Now, unless you're buying a round, I have other business to attend to." He waved the mortal away.

Sir Aleck left the tavern as quickly as he arrived. He reentered the palace, stealing through the passageways to reach his quarters without being seen. He exited into the hallway near his rooms, his spirits buoyed by his conversation with Heabel. The look on his Second's face, who stood at attention outside Aleck's door, gave him pause.

"Sir," the man began upon seeing his commander. He wrung his hands before continuing, "The Queen requests your presence urgently. She's been waiting hours. I couldn't find you."

'I'll handle the Queen," Aleck replied gently. He placed a hand on the man's shoulder. "Get some rest. This will all be over tomorrow." He gave the man a reassuring squeeze before turning in the direction of the Queen's chambers, his smile returning at the thought of his beloved.

Sir Aleck found Queen Isadore hunched over a large map of the city and the nearby plains. Her amber hair hung loosely, framing her face. He stared, love struck, as he always was, until she became aware of his scrutiny.

"Where have you been?" she spat, standing and folding her arms across her chest. "Tomorrow those two *kings* enter the city. Either I choose tonight or they both attack. I thought I could count on my general to be at my side to plan our defenses. But no, he's off doing Gods know what, while I'm left bereft of his council." Her blue eyes stared daggers, looking like shards of ice. However, her lips twitched towards a smile, spoiling it.

Aleck crossed the stone floor without speaking. He pulled his Queen into his arms, kissing her soundly. When he finally released her, she smacked him. "I suppose I deserve that," he said, rubbing his jaw.

Her face softened fully. "You know I can never stay angry with you. But. Where were you?" She rested her head against his chest.

"Ensuring our victory tomorrow," Aleck said. Isadore looked up into his eyes. "Let those chiefs in with their honor guard. Neither will leave alive unless they relinquish all claims to the throne. And to you."

"How?" she asked, hope lighting her face for the first time since the two armies appeared on her doorstep. When her husband died, she knew it was a matter of time before someone came calling.

"I cannot tell you, my Queen. But send them a message tonight. Tell them to enter through the Winds Gate. It has a large enough courtyard to accommodate my plan." Aleck pushed a lock of her hair aside, cupping her cheek affectionately.

Isadore pulled back to look at the city map, though she held fast to his hand. "Why that gate? If they choose to attack, it is a straight path to the castle. What are your plans to defend the road?"

"I will meet them just inside the gates. My men will clear all the civilians away from the area. Then I will end this once and for all. I need you to trust me."

"I do trust you, though your plan sounds foolhardy," she replied. She watched the intensity in his eyes. "I better send those messages as you plan. Are you sure about this? It seems dishonorable to plan a sneak attack." Worry caused little wrinkles around her sky-blue eyes. "Once they are inside the walls, I fear it won't end except in blood."

"They will have their chance to end this without bloodshed," Aleck said soothingly. "You have my word."

Isadore watched him go. "I hope not your blood, at least," she said to herself.

The morning dawned clear and bright. The slight breeze carried the salty scent of the sea clear to the windows of Sir Aleck's chambers on the south side of the castle. His Second helped him don the armor slowly, careful to check each strap and buckle for a proper fit. He replayed his conversation with Heabel, as he prepared his mind for the coming battle. He knew the enemy would attack when he issued his challenge, but he trusted in his love for his Queen to protect him.

A knock at his door dragged him from his thoughts. A Guard Captain opened the door and poked his head through before he could reply.

"Sir Aleck, the men are assembled, but we're going to have to move fast to get into positions around the gate. Many, however, would rather take the battle outside the city than fight within the walls." He paused; his hands clenched around his riding gloves. He lowered his gaze to the floor. "Forgive me for questioning your orders, Sir."

"I understand the men being wary of my instructions. We've never shied away from a fight before. I'll be down in a moment." After the Captain left, he faced his Second. "I need you to hold them to their oaths when I order them to remain and guard the castle." Aleck watched confusion turn to realization when the man's eyes returned to his. "The Queen must be kept safe if my plan fails. Can you do that for me?"

The man saluted, fear and admiration warring in his voice as he replied, "On my life and honor, no harm shall come to the Queen while there is still breath in my body."

"By Sotestari, I pray you don't have to test that oath," Aleck whispered after him. He finished donning his armor, strapped his sword and shield to his back, then went in search of his Queen. Isadore was the only person who could convince his men to disobey his orders, and he needed her to understand what he planned. At least, as much of it as he could tell her.

He found her in the same study, staring at the same map. The way the light played along her hair brought joy to his heart. He felt it fill him, resonating with the new magic within his armaments. The warmth and strength wrapped around him like his beloved's embrace. She raised her head from the maps. She smiled as their eyes met, but Aleck could see the worry hiding in her eyes. "My Queen," he said, bowing before he approached.

She took his hand and held it in both of hers. "Are you sure this plan of yours will work?"

"That's why I need to talk to you," he replied.

Her eyes clouded further. "What's wrong? What aren't you telling me?"

"I need you to trust me." He held tight to her hand. "I'm leaving the men here to protect you if something goes wrong. I'm going to challenge these 'kings' and put an end to this once and for all."

"That's suicide!" Queen Isadore tried to pull her hands from his. "I won't allow it. I order you to take the soldiers with you."

Aleck held onto her, his gaze locking with hers. He leaned in and kissed her as fiercely as he ever had in their stolen moments since the King's death. "Trust me. Please."

Isadore's heart raced from the heat in his kiss and she almost missed what he said. "Of course, I trust you."

"You must, if my plan is to work. I need to know the men stayed here to protect you. I need to know you're safe."

She nodded resignedly. "I will hold them to their positions with all my power."

Aleck kissed her again, tenderly this time. "Thank you. Wait for me here." With a final squeeze of her hands, he turned and marched from the room.

As the door shut behind him, Isadore hugged her arms to herself. She bit her lip in worry. "Surely he's riding to his death. Why didn't I just marry him?" She chastised herself. "Would the people allow it?"

Aleck rode alone through the streets to meet the heads of the armies. When he reached the courtyard, he signaled the two men to open the gate. Chain rattled, wood and iron creaked as the giant doors swung out. Two columns of men on horseback waited outside. He reminded himself of his station, Knight of the Talon, Lord General of Bealck.

The Talon whispered a prayer, "Sotestari, God of warriors, please guide my blade this day." He motioned his horse forward to meet them.

'King' Graeben entered through the gates first. His horse was stocky and dark, like its rider. The man looked over the courtyard as his honor guard flanked him. He sneered at Aleck. "Where is my bride, boy? I didn't come all this way to be left in the cold. It's high time she warmed my bed."

Sir Aleck fumed, thankful his helmet covered his face, granting him time to compose his voice. "M'Lord. I have a proposition for you."

"The only proposition I'll hear is from that pretty little Queen of yours. Now run along and tell her to prepare." Graeben spurred his horse forward. He jerked the reins when Aleck's sword cleared its scabbard.

The Talon pointed the blade at Graeben's chest. "You'll hear me out or die where you stand." Aleck waited for the men to calm their fidgety horses. The tension thickened with each heartbeat as Graeben's men looked for archers in windows and on rooftops. "I challenge your entire honor guard. Here in this courtyard. My steel against all of theirs, then yours. If you relinquish this campaign, I will spare your life and allow you to return to your people."

Graeben laughed for several moments while his men drew their weapons. He raised a hand when the first of them started forward. "I will dispatch this pathetic knight myself. Keep Dorgran waiting outside." Graeben's sword rang loudly as he pulled it from its sheath on his horse's side. "Be a shame to waste a good horse. Shall we dismount?" He punctuated his question by swinging his thick leg over and stepping down from his horse. One of his men walked his horse forward and grabbed the reins of his liege's stallion.

Aleck nodded acquiescence to his opponent's terms. Once dismounted, he whispered a command to his mount.

The highly trained war stallion trotted over near a small fountain and started to drink from the water. Aleck turned his attention to Graeben, who began to circle him.

"I'm going to take great pleasure in putting your head on a pike for the Queen to view while she becomes my wife," Graeben said as he paced his opponent. "Or would you rather be alive when I make her mine?"

"This is your last chance to surrender your claims and go home, Graeben," Aleck said calmly. He smiled as he feigned a strike to the bigger man's left. When Graeben went for it, Aleck spun on his heel. His blade passed a hair's breadth from the man's neck.

They two men circled each other again. Their swords clashed several times without either gaining an advantage. Their deadly dance went on for several minutes before Graeben said, "I tire of this game." He roared and charged.

Aleck shifted his weight, using his opponent's momentum to knock him from his feet. Aleck stood over the bigger man with his blade pointed down. "This is the end of your reign." Aleck pulled back the blade and drove it deep into Graeben's chest. The man's sword clattered to the ground.

"My King," several of the men on horseback yelled as they charged Aleck.

Aleck planted a boot in Graeben's chest and pulled his sword free. He dropped into a crouch and whistled to his horse as the first of the honor guard came within range. As his armored war horse crashed into the back of the men, he began cutting the men from their horses. A sound by the gates pulled his focus for just a moment as Dorgran and his men charged through the unblocked gate on foot and headed straight for the palace.

The momentary shift in Aleck's gaze allowed two of Graeben's men to strike, knocking him from his feet. They slid from their mounts, intent on finishing the job, when Aleck's horse barreled into them. The Talon regained his feet and sword and finished the enemy with swift cuts. As the pool of blood around him expanded and the fallen men's last sounds quieted, Aleck mounted his horse. He spurred towards the castle, giving chase to Dorgran and his soldiers. He knew the plainsmen were as fast on their feet as a horse, but this wasn't the rolling fields they normally stalked.

Several bodies of Bealck soldiers lay strewn across the entryway to the palace and Aleck paused long enough to whisper a prayer to Sotestari to watch over the souls of his men. A half dozen of Dorgran's men also lay dead and dying, bringing a smile to the general's face. He dismounted and let his horse wander to return to the stables. He took a deep breath before proceeding into the castle.

Aleck followed the signs of battle through the hallways and staircases until he reached the hall containing the royal apartments. Hearing the sounds of a pitched battle ahead, he stepped behind a tapestry and into a secret corridor. The darkened and dusty interior threatened to make him sneeze as he pressed on toward the Queen's chambers. Voices came to him through the cracks in the stone when he reached his destination.

"Queen Isadore, how lovely to find you right where you should be," Dorgran's baritone voice chilled Aleck's blood. There was no sound of fighting from the other side of the passage Aleck stood in.

"You will leave now," Isadore stated firmly, though her voice betrayed a measure of fear. "Leave my kingdom forever or face the wrath of the Talon."

"Your precious general is likely soaking the courtyard in his blood as we speak," Dorgran replied. "When my men and I went past, he was on foot, facing the whole of Graeben's honor guard. Was a shame, I didn't get to kill that fat half giant dog myself, but such is the way of fate. I suppose the Talon gets that honor, but I get the spoils."

"Aleck is dead?" Isadore's voice stuttered over the words, her heart breaking.

"Likely," Dorgran replied. "If not, my men will finish

him off. I may spare his life if you'll agree to my terms."

"You'll let him live if I marry you? You'll stop this bloodshed? Stop killing my people?" Isadore's voice came out in a rush.

"But of course. They would be my people if I were King," Dorgran said. "Will you be my Queen then?"

"I have no choice but to accept your gracious offer to save my people," Isadore replied, her words almost too soft to reach Aleck's ears where he fumbled with the latch.

Aleck couldn't believe she surrendered. He felt his shoulders sag as the weight of losing Isadore crept into his heart. Sounds of footsteps crossing from stone to carpet reached Aleck's ears before Dorgran spoke again, "Now I will take what is mine. Men, slaughter the rest of Bealck's troops and begin bringing the rest of ours into the city. Do not disturb us until I send word."

Aleck rushed through the false wall as soon as it opened. He raised his blade, racing toward his beloved when arms wrapped around him. Several of Dorgran's men grappled the knight, his sword was knocked from his hand and kicked to the side where it thunked against a wooden chest. Someone ripped his helmet off before they knocked him to the ground.

"I knew you would show up eventually," Dorgran said. He pulled Isadore against him. "Your Queen has just consented willingly. Come quietly and I will let you live out your days in my dungeon."

Aleck struggled, believing in the magic the Heabel had imbued his armor with. Dorgran's men held him down, overwhelming him through sheer force of weight at first. He started to rise, lifting all of them with him as the magic born of his love for his Queen flowed through him.

Isadore watched one of Dorgran's men draw a long slender blade and drive it into Aleck's arm, causing him to falter and land flat on his chest. As the soldier removed the knife and repositioned it at Aleck's throat, her heart fell. She looked up into Dorgran's face. She pulled the man's head down and kissed him.

The sight shook Aleck to his soul. He felt his strength falter, the magic leaving him. "No, Isadore. Don't," he mumbled in disbelief. One of Dorgran's men silenced him with a kick to the side of his head. Conscious, but barely, Aleck looked on as Dorgran pushed Isadore onto the bed.

He pulled the straps and discarded his breastplate before turning to his men. "After I'm through here, take him outside and put his head on a pike at the gates. Bealck has a new King." The soldiers pulled Aleck to his feet, holding him to watch. As Dorgran approached Isadore, she rose to a sitting position and drove a dagger into his stomach. She twisted the blade, bringing it upward to slice him open from bowels to lungs.

"Bealck will have no King except one I choose. Aleck is ten times the King you could ever be," Isadore said as she kicked at the taller man. She tried to backpedal away across the bed, but Dorgran grabbed an ankle. She screamed and kicked at his face, shattering his nose. He fell onto the edge of the bed beside her before sliding to the floor. His blood soaked into the plush carpeting under her bed.

Aleck's blurred vision took in Isadore's actions. "*She tricked him,*" he thought to himself. "*She truly loves me.*" Strength surged into him as the magic reawakened. Even the wound in his arm knitted back together as his head cleared. He roared, pulling the two holding his arms to crash into each other. He grabbed one of the long slender blades from the sheath on the man's hip and turned to the others. They squared off to attack when the Queen's door crashed open to reveal Aleck's Second and a couple more battered soldiers of Bealck. Dorgran's men raised their arms, knowing they were defeated.

As Isadore wrapped her arms around Aleck from behind, he nodded to his men. "Take them back to the gate. Tell them and Graeben's men that this is over. Go home, and their lives will not be forfeit. If they ever cross our borders again, then so help me, as long as breath remains in my body, I will destroy them, down to the last soldier."

"Yes, sir," his second replied, taking the arm of one of Dorgran's men. They hurried from the room, leaving Isadore and Aleck alone.

"My Queen," Aleck said, dropping the blade he held and turning to face her. "I promised no harm would come to you, and I failed."

"You didn't fail, though I feared you would die here in this room. I thought," Isadore said, shuddering. "I thought if I could buy you some time." She laid her head against his chest plate. The metal felt cool against her flushed skin as her breathing began to steady. A trickle of the armor's magic touched her, and she knew, beyond all doubt, how strong Aleck's devotion ran. "My King," she whispered.

"On this day, it is my honor to present to you, Queen Isadore and King Aleck," the herald pronounced from the gate to the assembled citizens. A great cheer shook the very stone of the city walls blocks away.

Aleck looked down from the balcony with Isadore at his side. As he scanned the mass of people in the square, he caught a shock of sandy blonde hair. The Heabel locked eyes with the new King, waving once before disappearing into the crowd. Aleck squeezed his beloved, his devotion swelling in his heart.

ABOUT THE AUTHORS

M.A. ROBERTS

Michael Roberts is a fantasy writer living in an old cowboy town on the edge of San Francisco Bay Area. He studied and taught philosophy but was always secretly writing about new worlds and adventures. After accidentally writing a novel instead of taking notes in class, he realized where his passion lies. Now he spends his free time playing in the worlds he creates and trying to convince people his playtime is actually hard work."

R.Q. WOODWARD

I am full of stories. I have been writing and revising for years, with the occasional query thrown in, but I am as of yet, unpublished. My M.A. in history and my love for reading instilled a sense of wonder in me for the unique perspectives of individuals in different societies, cultures, terrains, and time periods. I proofread professionally, am a captioner and sign language interpreter, a seamstress, and a full-time mom and vegan who can seriously chow down on some cookies.

LOWRY POLETTI

Lowry Poletti is a biology grad and aspiring veterinary student. Their interest in animal science and anatomy informs their writing which straddles the line between fantasy and horror. Their work appears in issue nine of Anathema magazine and in Vulture Bones magazine.

N.R. WILLIAMS

N. R. Williams is the author of The Treasures of Carmelidrium, Book 1 of The Chronicles of Gil-Lael. The Magic of Windlier Woods, Halloween Collection book 1 and 2. She lives in New Mexico with her husband and has two grown daughters and two grandchildren. When she was a child, she often pulled apart her mother's tulips, looking for faeries. You can find many faerie stories in the pages at the top on her blog.

http://authornrwilliams.com/

MARK J. SCHULTIS

Community leader. Particle physicist. International Assassin. Mark J Schultis is none of these. He wrote his first story in elementary school and has spent a lifetime keeping that childhood passion of storytelling alive, studying theatre and filmmaking before eventually earning his writing degree from the University of Pittsburgh. A perpetual night owl and pizza connoisseur, Mark was born and raised in Pittsburgh, Pennsylvania where he lives with his wife and their two children.

BETHANY A. PERRY

Bethany has had many lifetimes - one in the American South, one in the American West, and one both before and after sobriety. She's always had a passion for reading and writing, and when she's not working, hanging with her kids or partner or pets, she's likely at the computer, writing. Poetry, horror, fantasy, sci-fi, you name it. If it's got an off-beat twist, she's probably into it. Her debut novel, Reclamation, a sci-fi horror story about life after the zombie apocalypse and the Cure, and its sequel, Reclamation 2: Revolution, are both available wherever books are sold. Book 3, and the concluding chapter of the trilogy, is scheduled for release in the summer of 2021. She also has a contemporary fantasy novel entitled Give Me Grace coming from NineStar Press in 2021. If she were in front of you, she'd tell you to read a book. But also that a little TV is OK too, as long as it's Supernatural or Star Trek.

R.A. MEENAN

R. A. Meenan lives in her own private world of elemental magic and dragon A.I.s, cultivating a love of the weird, the wild, and the whimsical. When she's not sailing through space, she teaches college English students, hoping to rekindle the love of the written word.

BRANDON FIFE

Brandon Fife is a Junior High Spanish teacher who lives in Cheyenne, Wyoming with his wife, six children and a portly chocolate Labrador retriever named "Moose". His story "A Web of Vice" was published by the website Every Day Fiction in May of 2017. He has completed one novel (alas unpublished) and is currently laboring away on its sequel.

M.D. WEATHER

Originally from Rochester NY, M. D. Weather now resides in sunny (rainy) Orlando FL, where she enjoys writing, gaming, crocheting, and being a reptile-mom. Through her writing, Weather hopes to inspire fellow Autistic and neurodivergent adults to find their voices and reach for their dreams.

IGNACIO R. LIMÓN

Ignacio is a trans and Latinx Pacific Northwest author studying nursing in the Southwest. When he isn't writing or studying profusely, he can be found listening to music or doing arty things. On top of trying to find ways to streamline or declutter his life, he enjoys vegging out with a good book.

SUSAN ESCHBACH

Author, legal secretary, journalist, educator, conference planner. Susan Eschbach has worn many professional hats, none as challenging—or as fun—as writing science fiction. Growing up in Kansas City, she dreamed of traveling to distant planets. That was never possible, so she travels vicariously through her characters. Her writing experiences began in elementary school in 4-H, and years later led to a position as assistant editor of a small newspaper. She embarked on her first novel in 2008 at the insistence of a close friend and members of her critique group, Mid-South Writers. Susan has two books published by Oghma Press: A Trial by Error and Man On The Fringe, both available on Amazon and BarnesandNoble.com.

CLEMENTINE FRASER

Clementine Fraser lives in New Zealand with two boisterous sons and a giant doofus rescue dog. In her day job, she teaches teenagers to love history. Her passion for history and social justice influence many aspects of her life and filter into her writing. An avid fantasy reader from childhood, it is worlds of magic and romance that capture her imagination and make it sing. She writes romantic fantasy with lyrical description and strong characters, exploring the acceptance of self and the concept of choice, in a variety of immersive worlds and time periods.

ANDREW M FERRELL

Andrew M. Ferrell is a lifelong fantasy and science fiction lover who lives in NorthEast Wisconsin with his wife and three children, plus two attention seeking dogs. He splits his time between a factory day job, family commitments, his own writing, and running a small press. He currently has two full length novels and a novella published and can be found occasionally blogging on his site.

http://www.andrewmferrell.com

·

THE SCI FI & FANTASY WRITERS' GUILD